PHOENIX SECONDARY READERS LIBRARY

A Burst of Birdsong

PHOENIX SECONDARY READERS SERIES

1. Mwene's Rough Day — Charles O. Okoth
2. Imani and the Missing Mace — Kinyanjui Kombani
3. Shiundu and the Drugs Syndicate — Charles O. Okoth
4. The Secret Fort — Ngumi Kibera
5. The Great Siege of Fort Jesus — Valerie Cuthbert
6. Dragon's Flames — Patrick Kimiti
7. The Secrets of the Lizard — Patrick Kimiti
8. Shiundu and the Strange Sect — Charles O. Okoth
9. Pamela the Probation Officer — Cynthia Hunter
10. Truphena Student Nurse — Cynthia Hunter
11. Truphena City Nurse — Cynthia Hunter
12. The Circle of Revenge — David M. Mwaurah
13. Mystery of the Red Mountain — John K. Kariuki
14. The St. Helena Conspiracy — Kahiu Mbugua
15. Children of the Red Fields — Monica de Nyeko
16. Company 18 — Macharia Magu
17. Move on, Trufosa! — Imali J. Abala
18. The Disinherited — Imali J. Abala
19. Operation Kamaliza — Munro Katui
20. The Miracle Merchant — Wahome Mutahi & Wahome Karengo

and more .... many more

A Burst of Birdsong

Erick Livumbazi Ngoda

 **PHOENIX PUBLISHERS, NAIROBI**

First published in 2018 by
Phoenix Publishers Ltd.
Mellow Heights, Ngara Road.
P.O Box 30474-00100,
Nairobi.

© Text: Erick Livumbazi Ngoda, 2018
© Design and illustrations: Phoenix Publishers Ltd., 2018

ISBN 9966 47 909 0

Printed by:
Autolitho Limited
Enterprise Road,
P.O. Box 73476 Enterprise Rd,
Nairobi.

For

Westgate and for Kofi Awuonor

1

Will they forever be earthbound

Will they rise?

Can their feet leave the ground

Shall their wing

 beat again?

Will they be forever flightless

Will they rise?

Will their struggle remain relentless

Can their being

its essence regain?

Will they soar the skies

Will they rise?

As the eagle's wing flies,

Can they be restored to their height?

 ~Birdsong

"M'ma! These cracks in my heels are deep enough to hide a whole coin in! I should buy some *akala*, my slippers are worn right through...I could as well be walking around barefoot!" Big Susy complained in her hoarse raspy voice. Kadesa, who always seemed angry with everyone and everything, pushed her away from the stone on which she had been scrubbing her heels and started scrubbing her own. Kadesa usually teased Big Susy that her voice was hoarse from way too much talking, which had an element of truth. Big Susy just bubbled and went on and on–she didn't seem to ever stop talking!

"Tell your Jemsi to buy you some simple rubber shoes, he works in Nairobi..." Kadesa said with a smug sniff as she turned one of her own heels deliberately so Big Susy could see how smooth it was.

Carol liked Big Susy much more than she did Kadesa. Big Susy was round and cuddly like an oversized teddy bear. She usually made everyone laugh and was always laughing herself and telling all sorts of funny stories all the time. The two women were quite the opposite of each other. Whereas Big Susy was the kind of person you wanted to hug and snuggle up to, Kadesa seemed so...sharp, cold and dangerous, like a broken bottle, knife or a sharp, rusted piece of metal. She was like something that cuts, hurts and makes someone bleed and feel pain. You wanted...needed to keep her as far away from you as possible. Big Susy was very dark-skinned and had a broad face with two chins, while on the other hand, Kadesa's light-skinned face was sharp, in every way that you looked at it. Her cheekbones seemed to be straining sharply against the taught skin of her face. Her nose was thin, sharp and slightly hooked like a hawk's beak. Carol always felt as if she was piercing right into her soul with her ever-angry eyes whenever she looked at her. Right then, Carol had been secretly amusing herself by watching Big Susy's plump body–especially her generous backside–jiggling vigorously as she tried with a lot of determination to scrub away the cracks in the rough skin of her heels on a small rock that was partly embedded in the ground. Most homes in the village had such stones on which people scrubbed their feet while washing. This was a sort of simple daily pedicure routine to help reduce *amaga*, the cracks that form in the hard, callused soles of people who walk barefoot most of the time.

By the way, only Carol called Susy 'Big', and even then only in her thoughts. She thought of Susy not as fat, but as cheerful, jolly, Santa Claus-big. This was one of the many things that endeared Big Susy to her so much.

Carol's thoughts were a secret place where only she went. A place where she carefully kept sweet memories and happy thoughts like special-occasion clothes, carefully folded and lovingly locked away. Most of the memories were from not very long ago when things had been so different, before everything suddenly changed. Kadesa was one of the problems that now made her world a difficult place to live in. She seemed to hate Carol's guts, not that Carol ever did anything to annoy her in any way. But then Kadesa didn't seem to like anyone at all anyway. The good thing was, whenever she had to be around Kadesa, Big Susy was always around too, to make her feel a bit safe and protected.

The three of them were washing their faces, arms, legs and feet from the same plastic basin of water. They had been weeding Madam Redempta's maize farm, a job for which they were usually paid two hundred shillings a day each. At sixteen, Carol was forced to do such casual jobs alongside grownups for the sake of her family; her mother, her brother Greg, who was thirteen, and their eight-year-old sister Paulette. She now had to think about everyone else before she thought about herself. They all looked up to her and depended on her to provide everything for them.

"You! Give me the stone!" Kadesa snarled at Carol. "Why are you staring into the air like that? Listening to the birds sing?"

Startled out of her thoughts, Carol quickly passed the pumice stone she had been scrubbing her feet with to Kadesa. She felt a mixture of embarrassment and anger at Kadesa's words.

It was so cruel for the woman to say such a thing to her; it was not Carol's fault that her mother was not very right in the head. The problems they had all gone through had made her sick, and they had no money at all to pay for the doctor and the medicine that she needed.

Her mother's condition had improved somehow when they had moved back to the village, but she was not the person she once was. Now everyone called her Lwa-Manyonyi, which means 'Song- of- birds' or 'Birdsong'. This was because she was always talking about the way the birds sang, putting words to the sounds the birds made. Some of these 'lyrics' were so funny that people laughed and made her repeat them again and again, over and over, which embarrassed Carol terribly. Most of these words she made up were in very good English, and this just made the village folk laugh even more. "How can a madwoman speak English?" they usually wondered loudly.

To them she was just a madwoman, and nothing else- a lowly creature to be mocked and laughed at. The sickness had reduced Carol's mother to a mere child mentally. Nothing remained at all of the high school English language and literature teacher who had always been so smartly dressed and perfectly made up, as Carol remembered her. Carol now had to force her mother to take a bath and change her clothes when they became too dirty. She constantly worried about her mother, fearing that something horrible would happen to her as she wandered about the village, or that perhaps one day she would wander off very far away where she would never be found.

That is how her life had become. Always worrying and thinking about her mother, her brother and sister. Greg had adjusted well to the village life, better than the rest of them. He could run along with their cousins and other village boys, climbing trees, throwing pebbles at birds and raiding their nests, scaring squirrels out of the bushes and doing all the other things they did. Paulette had been quite little when they had been in Nairobi, and she could barely remember how life was then. Somehow, she had grown old beyond her years.

Carol wished Paulette could experience the joy and fun she had when she was her younger sister's age. Back then, she had gone for holidays at the coast with their parents, shopped for designer clothes and expensive toys at upmarket malls in affluent parts of the city, visited the parks and other fun places... all the precious, joyful experiences of her childhood that were now neatly and lovingly kept in the treasure box that her memory was. The serious, unsmiling look on her younger sister's face made Carol so sad for the little girl who would probably never have any of the carefree fun and happiness that all children should have.

"Kaaro, let's get into the house and eat," Big Susy grabbed Carol's hand and almost dragged her into the house. "I hope that woman will give us enough food this time, people who have been working in the shamba need to eat not just taste food." She said this in a lower voice so that Madam Redempta's house help wouldn't hear her. Big Susy never stopped complaining about the food they were given whenever they worked at Madam Redempta's farm. She suspected that the househelp, Zinafa, kept for herself more of the food that they were supposed to be given.

Carol really, really needed the money she made from

weeding and doing other farm work for Madam Redempta and other well-off people around the village. However little the money was, it came in handy. Every cent had to be stretched thin to try and buy at least some of the bare essentials, and even then, it was never enough. It was quite the opposite of how things had been, just slightly more than a couple of years ago, when her mother was a high school teacher and her late father had been a banker. Then, all she did and was mostly required to do was wake up and go to school. Now it seemed like a pleasant dream that never even was!

She was now going to school again—Hillside Academy, which had just about ninety students. The entire school, that is. It had been started just a couple of years earlier by an elderly lady known to the locals as Madam Juliet, with the help of her daughter in Canada and one of her step-sons, who lived and worked as an architect in the United States. Madam Juliet was originally from Canada but had lived in the area for many years. Hillside mainly took in bright students from poor families around the village and even beyond, who were not required to pay much school fees. The problem was that the school had only four full-time teachers apart from Madam Juliet. There were two more teachers who taught in other schools, and could only be at Hillside for an hour or so twice or three times a week.

The students had to study on their own and tutor each other a lot of the time. Some were past school-going age, since they had been languishing at home for lack of school fees for a long time. Others had gone to school before, but had had to drop out for lack of fees and other problems, just like her. There was, for instance, Ebby Siaha who had been forced to drop out of school after a boy at the school she had attended made her pregnant. Forced to go and live with the boy and his parents, she had another baby before the first one could even walk. Her boyfriend's parents made her do too much backbreaking work besides mistreating her, so much so that she had finally gone back to her parents. And now Hillside had given her another chance to have a bright future. Most of the other students had similar sad stories to tell, and most of them were determined to make maximum use of the chance they were being given.

In the few months she had been at the school, Carol had struck a rapport with Madam Juliet. The elderly lady seemed to like her more than she did the other students. Perhaps it was because Carol was always so quiet and attentive, and more disciplined than the rest of the students. Or maybe Madam Juliet just felt pity for the painfully thin girl, who always seemed to be in some pain and torment that was deeper inside than anyone could ever reach and touch. After school, Carol would go to Madam Juliet's little house which was just a few metres away from the school to tidy it up for her and do the dishes and laundry, prepare her simple meals and run any other errands for her. She realised that what Madam Juliet paid her for the simple tasks was much more than she really deserved, but she needed all the help she could ever get.

"She didn't put any oil in the vegetable, see!" Carol was once again startled from her thoughts by Big Susy's not-so-low hoarse whisper, which must have carried to the kitchen where Zinafa was. She was showing Kadesa and Carol the small metal bowl that contained kale greens, with which they were to eat the *ugali*.

"Eat!" Kadesa hissed back at Big Susy. "Do you cook better food than this at your home?"

Carol didn't know what to say. She could see that it was true the vegetables looked simply boiled and unappetizing, but she didn't want to annoy Kadesa by agreeing with Big Susy.

"Perhaps you should go to Nairobi where your husband is, so that you will be eating well every day!" Kadesa arrogantly suggested.

"Which Nairobi are you talking about? It's got worse problems than here." Big Susy shrugged her shoulders as she fashioned a small mound of ugali with her fingers and put a dollop of the offensive kale on top of it.

"They live in hot little rooms made from *mabati* all round, they get so hot I tell you...and they don't even have toilets...," she popped the mound of ugali into her mouth, making her cheeks rounder and bulkier that they already were.

Carol couldn't help smiling at Big Susy's description of Nairobi. Which Nairobi had the woman been to?

"Jemsi wanted me and the children to go and live there, but I refused!" Big Susy continued through a mouthful of food, "So many houses close to each other, and M'ma! ...the stench!"

The way she said it made Carol giggle suddenly. Kadesa glared at her with a lot of disdain.

"So you find it funny? Is that the place you people used to live...and your father would come here and treat us like we were garbage? See? This world is round my dear...it went round, and it has come round!"

"Kadesa! Really, what is wrong with you?" Big Susy exclaimed in surprise. "Are these the things to tell a child?"

"The truth will always stand!"

Kadesa shrugged her shoulders and smugly put a bite-size piece of ugali into her mouth. It was obvious that she got a lot of pleasure from torturing and tormenting Carol...and indeed everyone else around her, the way she did.

"Don't mind her child...just eat your food...this is the way she usually is... here, have a bit of my *sukuma wiki*, it has some onion in it at least..."

Big Susy nodded towards her with pity on her wide face as she slid a bit of her vegetables into Carol's bowl with her plump sausage-like forefinger, while chewing and swallowing all along. That was how it always was when she was with the two —Kadesa looking for the worst words to hurt her with, and Big Susy offering her the better part of what she was eating and comforting words. Her kindness was like a breath of cool, soothing air over a hurting wound. For some reason, Big Susy always insisted on taking Kadesa along with her whenever she found a job around the village. It was usually the plump woman who sought out the jobs, and every weekend she would take Carol along so that she too 'could get something to put inside the stomach' as she put it.

Carol was not really affected much by Kadesa's words. She had heard worse. She had gone through quite a lot, mostly at other people's hands. What she was thinking about at the moment was how Big Susy had described Nairobi, where she had spent a good part of her childhood. But it was not in a place like Susy was describing. It had been a comfortable house with three bedrooms, and a bathroom with a tub and a shower. And that was the rented house in Komarock estate before they had moved to the house her parents had built in Syokimau.

All that was in the past now. Her dad was gone. They said he had problems with his heart, but others said it was suicide. The traumatic things that had happened to the family in such a short time were enough to make both possible. She had been so young, but even then, she had been fully aware of what both her parents had been going through. They had lost just about everything they owned during the sudden demolition done by the government.

"It is true as you keep saying...this world is round, Kadesa." Big Susy, chewing and swallowing a bit noisily as she talked, glanced sideways at Kadesa.

"You never know, perhaps this child you are tormenting will be married by your son. Who knows what plans God has in store for everyone?"

She shrugged her shoulders yet again. Kadesa made a disgusted face as if she was about to spit.

"That would never be God's plan, it would be the devil's!"

"The devil did not create people, he does not make plans for our lives." Big Susy continued with her argument.

Listening to the two women arguing, Carol suddenly realized something. If the world is indeed round, and everything comes around and goes around, then everything she and her family were going through would come to an end someday. Perhaps it really was in God's plan. All this was meant to happen, and the bad times would go round, so that good times could come round once more. Kadesa had meant for her words to hurt, but instead they had given her a ray of hope!

She could feel a tinge of joy—a ray of hope somewhere deep down inside her as she thought that. Kadesa's words were, in a way, like the confirmation she needed that all she had to do was to keep being strong, for herself and for her mother, brother and sister. To be strong and survive as they waited for that moment when what had gone round would come round again. She closed her eyes tightly, drew in a deep breath and slowly let it out again.

Big Susy's attention had already moved on, however. She was staring at the beautiful carvings and colourful paintings that were all around Madam Redempta's dining room.

"Rich people! I hear they spend a lot of money on such decorations, a small one like that could even cost a whole one thousand shillings!"

Carol again smiled to herself at the way Big Susy said that, pointing to a colorful painting of a mother in traditional garb suckling her infant while holding onto a calabash decorated with multi-colored beads. It was as if one thousand shillings was a very large amount of money to her!

Carol stopped herself from telling them that such a painting cost quite a lot more than that. Her father had had quite a number of paintings that he had bought from galleries and at art exhibitions. They had been exhibited all around their living room, which had been about three times larger than Madam Redempta's. The paintings had cost her dad such a lot of money—there was even one that he had bought for a quarter of a million Kenya shillings at an exhibition by a famous West African artist at the Alliance Française de Nairobi! He had loved art so much, but the entire collection had been destroyed the day the bulldozers came.

"This is why I said you are so mad, you too should be singing with the birds," Kadesa arrogantly told Big Susy. "How can a piece of paper with drawings like that cost a whole one thousand shillings?"

"It is me that is telling you!" Big Susy said firmly. "Jemsi used to work for an Indian who sold such carvings and drawings!" Her hoarse voice rose a bit higher as she said that. Carol glanced sideways at Kadesa. The lightness of the woman's skin made the several darker-coloured scars — one on her forehead and several others on her cheeks and the largest across the bridge of her nose—very visible. She had deep creases around her ever-angry mouth. Her sharp, beaky nose made her look even more like the witches in the animated movies that Carol used to love watching. Carol guessed that Kadesa must be around her mother's age; forty or slightly older. What made her so angry with everyone and everything?

"Oh, Jemsi... and is that the person who can tell people anything?" Kadesa said with a dismissive click of her tongue.

Carol could sense that even Big Susy was getting annoyed.

"What do you mean when you tell me that?" she asked in a low voice.

"I was just saying... it's not my fault that the truth hurts." Kadesa had that smug look on her face that she always put on whenever she succeeded in hurting someone. Carol had come to notice that the only thing that could really annoy Big Susy was when anyone talked ill of her Jemsi. Big Susy referred to the things that her husband told her time and again... like all the time! It was obvious that she loved him and believed in him so much, just the way Carol's parents had loved each other. She had noticed that even when she was very young. She was their first child, and she had more memories of the happier times than her brother and sister. She remembered when her father sometimes came home with bouquets of flowers for her mother, and would sometimes hug her and peck her on the cheek when they thought no one was watching.

It was entered on the death certificate that Carol carefully kept in a file with other important documents that what had caused his death was 'cardiac arrest'. Perhaps they should have written 'heartbreak'. The terrible events in the days before her father had died were enough to break anyone's heart—the same events that had made her mother snap when she couldn't cope anymore.

Now Carol fully realised that she was the head of the family, if there was any. She was the 'man' of the home. She had to keep all their lives going as best as she could. That is why she learned to work on the farms around the village besides the errands she ran for Madam Juliet after school and during the weekends. And whatever she did, she knew that she had to keep going to school one way or another, whatever it took. She had to pass the exams. That was one sure way out of her situation.

2

Not right now

But all in good time

What it takes is to tread the path

Where it takes will work itself out

Every beat brings its strength

With each flop, success is nearer

With time

Not right now,

but somewhere along the line.

~Birdsong

"Physics is a boy's subject. You should be good at English or literature and stuff like that," Saidi laughingly told Carol. He was obviously miffed—but in a good way—by the fact that Carol was so much better than him at Physics and Mathematics, indeed all the other science subjects. She always seemed to know much more than the rest of her class.

Okay, maybe that was because she had been to a big school in the city before she came to the village and joined Hillside.

"Who said that? Madam Juliet teaches Physics and Chemistry, and she is a woman," Carol protested.

"But she is a *mzungu*!" Saidi retorted.

"What about your cousin, Miss Sagala? She teaches Math and Physics!" Carol argued. Miss Munira Hussein Sagala was one of the part-time teachers who occasionally taught at Hillside.

"She is white on the inside," Saidi answered with a cheeky grin that made Carol laugh out loud.

Carol really liked Saidi, who was one of the brightest of the fifteen students in her class. She really didn't think of him as her boyfriend as such, but he always cheered her up her with his jokes and wisecracks. The only time she was totally happy, with every sad thought forgotten, was when she was chatting with Saidi. Tall, lanky and light-skinned, Saidi had slightly curly, very black hair and a sunny, cheeky grin on his face most of the time. Carol secretly thought he was very cute. People said that Saidi's grandmother had been an Arab woman; his grandfather had married her when he had lived and worked in Mombasa on the Kenyan coast.

Saidi was from the area's Muslim community who lived together in a cluster of mostly clay and iron sheet houses at the edge of Majengo shopping centre that everyone called 'Mjini'— the town. This was the home of very interesting and mysterious people who, to the rest of the villagers, lived in a fascinating world of their own that was straight off the pages of a storybook. The women went around all wrapped up and hooded in brightly colored *lesos* or mysterious, all-shrouding *buibuis* with just their eyes peeping out. Most of the men wore beautifully embroidered skull-caps and flowing snow-white *kanzu* robes. Many a myth and captivating tale was woven around Mjini and the people who lived there, but no one seemed to know which of these tales were true and which were not. Everybody just seemed to have heard them from someone else.

Most members of the community regarded the people from Mjini with suspicion, and maybe quite a bit of disdain. Perhaps because they belonged to a different faith and did most things differently from the way others did them. People also said that girls from Mjini were not very good, and they did bad things with men for money. It was also rumoured that apart from the illegal liquor that was openly sold in some of the houses, some people from the community also sold hard drugs. Some of the other students even openly laughed at her friendship with Saidi.

"Why do you like hanging around that boy from Mjini?" her cousin Jose, who also went to Hillside once asked her. "He will make you lose your way, and do you know they sell drugs there? Or perhaps you have even started taking them too," he added, looking at her suspiciously.

Carol had completely ignored him. She knew from experience that whenever Jose started a quarrel with her, and she reacted to it, he always told his mother—her Aunt Rispa — about it. Then she would go over to the house and insult Carol over it later.

"What are you thinking about now?" Saidi's voice roused her from her thoughts, "the law of diminishing returns? Or you are coming up with your own theorem?" he laughingly teased in his low, deep voice.

"Feeling threatened, are we? Why don't you come up with your own theorem?" Carol teased back, grinning warmly. She liked the way Saidi's Adam's apple pulsed slowly in his throat when he talked. It was so hypnotizing...and it made her all breathless although she could not understand why. Or why she always felt so warm inside and happy whenever she even thought about him.

"Why are you staring at my neck that way? You are making me nervous!" Saidi covered his neck with the exercise book that he was holding.

"When you are light-skinned, you should be scrubbing you neck properly while bathing, your neck is so dirty!" she teased him softly. Believing her, a look of horror and embarrassment spread across his face and both his mouth and eyes opened a bit wider. It made Carol laugh out loud.

"You should see the look on your face!" she widened her own eyes and opened her mouth to mimic him, "I was only teasing, come on!"

They both laughed, Saidi a bit nervously.

"You are such a naughty little girl, do you know that?" he made as if to slap her with his book. Then Carol had this urge to look around. She caught a few of their classmates staring at them and whispering to each other, most of them with amused grins on their faces.

"Oh no, now you have made them say things about us," Carol whispered nervously.

"They have already said everything anyone could ever say, what else could they add? That you are being spoilt by the boy from Mjini or that I am being ruined by the city girl?"

He laughed as he said that, but Carol felt a bit embarrassed. All the same, it was true that they had that in common — the stigma of being who they were. She was the daughter of a madwoman — a 'spoilt' city girl and he was... well, from Mjini! Perhaps that was the bond that bound them together as much as it set them aside from everyone else.

The students had been relaxing in the little yard in front of the school during recess, after taking the cup of porridge that the school offered during recess as part of their feeding program. For some of the students, what they ate at school was the only decent meal they had each day. Hillside Academy did not have a real playground where the students could play games or engage in other extra-curricular activities. It was in a residential area and had been a partitioned building that Madam Juliet's late husband had previously rented out.

Juliet lived in a small three-roomed house just next to the school. People around the village said that she had met her husband, Hezbon, when he had been studying in her home country, Canada. They had fallen in love and married there. What she didn't know then was that Hezbon already had a wife and five children back home. Hezbon's culture allowed a man to have more than one wife, but apparently he was not sure Juliet would understand if he explained that to her.

Big Susy always made it seem so funny whenever she related the story of the drama that followed when the two came back to Kenya on the completion of Hezbon's studies. She made it seem as if she had been there and personally witnessed it. Hezbon's Kenyan wife had been very angry, shouting at Hezbon to 'take back that woman he had brought home', and poor Juliet had stood there totally baffled, looking on and understanding nothing of what was happening.

Hezbon had to lie to her that the wife was his late brother's widow, who was complaining that he had not been taking care of her properly as tradition required. It was quite some time before Juliet learned the truth, but by then, she couldn't just turn on her heel and go back home. She had burned bridges and chosen the man she loved over her own family and a lot of other things. Her father had been very much against her marrying a foreign student she knew next to nothing about. And so she had lived for almost fifty years among her husband's community.

She and her husband's other wife had become fast friends over the years, long after she discovered the truth. She had even paid school and college fees for her step-children. She had only one daughter, who now lived and worked in her mother's homeland Canada — in fact in the very place that Juliet had been born and raised in — Duncan on Vancouver Island.

Now Madam Juliet's husband and his other wife had passed on, but her step-children still liked her a lot, and regarded her as a parent. Juliet and one of her step-sons, Kenneth, had decided to convert the old building into a school for poor bright students, and her daughter Lindsey, or Ondisa as her dad had always called her, supported the project by sending home money for the running expenses from her own savings and also from donors that she contacted in Canada. Now people like Saidi and Carol who had absolutely no way of paying for high school had a chance.

Minutes after entering the classroom, the students stood up to greet Madam Juliet, who briskly walked in with her file and some text-books. She was tall but a bit stooped, perhaps because of age. Her long hair had a lot of grey strands, but you could still see that it had been a rich auburn. She always had it brushed back and secured into a tight chignon at the back of her head

She was somewhere in her seventies, but still quite active and cheerful a lot of the time. The students enjoyed her lessons very much. She talked freely with Carol and confided so many personal things to her. Perhaps she was just lonely inside. She hardly interacted much with people, preferring to live a reclusive and private life. She once confided in Carol that she had been a teacher most of her life, in Canada, then in Ghana where she volunteered for a while before going back home to continue with her studies. It was during this period that she had met Hezbon.

"You may take your seats," she said in her soft but chirpy voice. The students looked forward to her lessons because she always had wonderful stories to tell in between the real lessons. Plus, they were mostly so grateful that she had given them the chance they would never have got elsewhere.

"Why can't she just stay at home and rest?" Saidi had once asked during one of the long conversations he usually had with Carol. "She doesn't earn anything from teaching at Hillside and I really think she has helped enough people already in her life!"

"I guess she is just so used to working every day that she doesn't know any other way to live except by teaching and helping people," Carol had suggested.

Juliet was an enigma, a wonder to many people, and a hero to the young people who she gave the chance they may never have had. When Carol and her family had relocated to the village, she assumed that school was out of the question. She had imagined that now all she would do was watch over her sick mother and siblings. Even that, she did not know how she was going to do. Up to that time, her parents had always provided everything she ever needed. All she had had to think about was finishing high school and scoring a grade that would enable her to join medical school, which had been her dream from as far back as she could remember. Her favourite game as a toddler had been nursing her 'sick' dolls, taking their temperature — the way she saw the nurses and doctors at the hospital do when she went for checkups — with a thermometer she had made herself from a piece of stick and listening to their chests with a stethoscope fashioned from a bottle top and a length of thread.

For a while, she had been convinced that her dream had been rendered impossible by circumstances. Madam Juliet had given her hope and helped her to see the sun through the dark clouds that had suddenly filled her sky. She had taught Carol to do all that she could do as she waited for that wind of change that must someday sweep away those dark clouds and bring out the warmly smiling face of the sun again.

In the months that Carol had lived in the village, she had learnt so many things about the simple way the people led their lives. One of this is the way most women kept one faggot or brightly glowing piece of firewood of the fire on which they cooked breakfast in the morning. This, they covered up with some embers and a lot of ashes. They called it *kufumbika*. The faggot remained alive and burning under the ashes until later in the day when it was needed to start another fire. Then the ashes were scraped away and *vusaasu*, splinters and pieces of firewood, piled over it before it was fanned to make another fire.

The love for science subjects was the glowing faggot which Carol had kept under the ashes of worries and sorrow and the sudden traumatizing events that had threatened to destroy her life and those of her entire family. At Hillside Academy, this faggot had been fanned alive once more, and she would sit in a class with books on her desk and a teacher at the front, and the fire of the dream she had thought was fated to die would burn fiercely, its heat defying the glum circumstances that surrounded her. Now she had hope; something she woke up every morning thinking about. A destination at which she knew she would arrive someday, however long it may take.

3

If it is morning yet

Why is it dark still?

If there is a sun

Why is there a chill?

Where is the fun

Why do we sing

among the dewy diamonds?

   ~Birdsong

"There was a bird outside in the hedge this morning and it kept saying,

> Good boy toto!

Bring back toto!

Good job toto!" Carol's mum said. "I think it has a very good baby bird that it really loves!"

She was staring into the roof of the house with that blank look she sometimes had on her face. Carol thought it was some kind of barrier that, in the process of blocking away the intense pain and suffering the woman had tried to escape from, had completely blanked out her personality as it had been.

"Muuum...birds don't talk..." Paulette said, with the serious pouty look she always had on her face.

"Of course they don't talk, they sing!" her mother looked at her with a sudden fierce spark in her eyes. Listening to Paulette and their mother seemed to Carol like listening to two children of the same age.

"You have to be able to talk to sing!" Paulette insisted.

"I wish people could just sing and not talk," her mother said. A pained expression drifted across her face again as she said that. Whenever memories of some of the things she had experienced crossed her mind, Carol's mother would seem to clam up inside herself. Carol had noticed that because she always watched her mother very closely. The roles had reversed and her mother had become the vulnerable child that had to be watched over all the time.

She slowly stood up and went into the kitchen where she had been boiling some water for her mother's bath. She tipped the water from the saucepan it was in into a plastic basin.

"Time for your bath; come on!" she told her mother. She could clearly remember years back when she had been a kid, and her mother would tell her exactly the same thing she was now telling her.

"I'm not dirty. I bathed this morning," her mother argued in a stubborn voice.

"No you did not, you have not taken a bath for two days Mum. Put on this leso while I take the water out to the bathroom," Carol said firmly. She had to be firm with her mother as with a stubborn child. Even Paulette was less trouble than their mother. In fact the child was usually more serious and grown-up than a child really should be. Carol took the basin full of warm water, a towel and a bar of soap and carried them out to the small corrugated iron enclosure at the back of their house, which they used as a bathroom.

"Come on, before the water cools down...you don't want to catch a cold," she told her mother, who was looking at the leso in her hands with a lot of dislike. By the time Carol had put the water inside the makeshift bathroom and come back into the room, her mother had tied the leso under her armpits and got rid of the filthy skirt and the equally grubby, torn blouse she had been wearing. Sometimes the clothes she wore had to be burned. They just could not be cleaned. Carol always wondered how her mother got her clothes so dirty or all torn up! She could put on a perfectly clean set of clothes in the morning, but by evening, they would be grimy rags shredded beyond repair.

Carol had learned to take care of her mother right from the day she had collapsed while teaching at school. The doctor at the hospital she had been taken to explained that she had gone into depression. That had been about two months after her father's death. For almost three weeks, Carol's mother had lain silently on her hospital bed, saying nothing at all. All she ever did was stare at the ceiling. Once in a while, she would get what seemed like violent seizures that made her stiffen and jerk about on her bed. The doctor called these 'panic attacks'.

As the hospital bill increased by the day and her mother didn't look like she was making any progress in her recovery, the doctor had called her and requested for a meeting. She had only been fourteen, a mere child, but there hadn't been anyone else the doctor could talk to. Carol clearly remembered Dr. Gichohi's snow-white lab-coat and the shiny stethoscope around his neck, his bald pate and the worried frown on his broad, chocolate-coloured face.

"Don't you have any grown-up relative we can discuss this with?" the doctor had asked. Carol had thought about her Aunt Gracie, her mother's elder sister who lived in Ofafa Jericho, where her mother and her family had been raised. Aunt Gracie was the only living grown-up relative on her mother's side that she knew. Her mother had had a brother too, but her Uncle Josh had died a few years back, when Carol had been much younger. Uncle Josh's wife had died a year before him. Both had died from complications resulting from AIDS. Their two children now lived with Auntie Gracie, who had three children of her own. Carol, even then, knew that her Auntie Gracie really had too much on her plate to be expected to assist much. All she had as a means of earning an income was a stall where she sold vegetables, fruit and other green groceries. That and whatever she got from selling illegal liquor that she got from upcountry and secretly sold – mostly in the evenings. She also took some of the liquor she sold, and she was quite a sight to behold when she did.

Carol's mother had once told her that Aunt Gracie had been a very brilliant student when she was younger. She had once had a bright future ahead of her until she had been expelled from university after being accused of instigating some of her fellow students to riot. From then on, her life had taken a downward spiral. Carol's mum had been the shining light of the family, excelling in school and college, getting a job as a high school teacher straight after college and marrying a successful man. She had taken care of the entire family, supporting them as much as they could; including both their parents until they had passed on. Then in one single day her life had suddenly crumbled to bits, literally.

"It is pointless for your mother to keep staying here," the doctor had explained to Carol when she had convinced him that she there wasn't anyone else he could speak to.

"Her recovery—if she ever recovers, depends on her. Right now, she has withdrawn into a world where no one can reach her. Only she can decide to come back to us," he had explained. The condition, according to the doctor, was a tactic of her mother's mind to escape the unpleasant unexpected circumstances that she had suddenly had to go through. The sudden loss of the house then her husband must have been too much for her mother to bear, and so her mind had simply shut down.

Staying with Aunt Gracie in her crowded two-roomed house in Ofafa Jericho had not even been an option, and there were no other relatives the family could stay with in Nairobi. It was up to Carol to make the decisions. She had suddenly become the head of the family. When things had started going the wrong way, Carol had woken up to the harsh reality that the hordes of people who had frequented their house had not even been relatives or friends as she had thought- not a single one of the 'aunties' and 'uncles', some of whom had so fondly and lovingly referred to her as 'sweetie'. Everyone had suddenly become so distant! There didn't seem to be even one relative in sight to turn to!

And that is how they had ended up in the village, living in the small house that had been the 'boy's hut' which her father and his brothers had once lived in during their childhood. Her father had concentrated on developing the plot he had bought in Syokimau, and completing the house, which Carol understood had cost about seven million shillings to complete. He had wanted to build a village house for the family once he was through with the house in Syokimau, but fate had had other plans for him.

"Carol! The water is too hot!" her mother called from the bathroom. She quickly poured some cold water into another basin and carried it out to her mother.

"Scrub the back of the neck properly with the loofah", Carol told her mother in a low voice as she pushed the other basin of water into the bathroom. She recalled grimly again that that was exactly the kind of thing her mother would have told her twelve or so years ago when she was just learning to take a bath by herself. She went back into the house just in time to save the ugali from burning. She deftly turned it before putting it onto a plate. She noticed that Paulette was very sleepy and about to doze off.

"Hey sleepyhead!" she playfully poked her younger sister, "the food is ready!"

Paulette yawned wearily and stretched.

"Now where is that boy?" Carol wondered loudly. Greg was never inside the house. But Carol couldn't blame him. The tiny two roomed hut was not a very nice place for an energetic ten year old to be. He was mostly out at their Uncle Jacob's house a few metres away. Carol didn't like him going there, but she couldn't make him stop doing so. Uncle Jacob had not been on very good terms with their father, and he had never pretended to like his late brother's wife and children. Carol had overheard someone say that Jacob, who was younger than her dad, had a grudge against her dad because he thought her dad should have helped him more with his own children's education.

But Greg and his cousins John and Kevin were inseparable. Perhaps the blood they shared drew them to each other even when the grownups tried so hard to pull them apart. Greg usually went to his uncle's to watch TV and do his homework alongside his cousins. Carol often wondered whether her family would have had more support from her father's family had he been closer to them while he had lived. It seemed as if they had never liked him much! When she thought about it, she remembered that they never visited much when her family had lived in Nairobi. She once in a while saw some distant relatives, but never her father's immediate family.

She had somehow learned that her father's family did not like her mother and had been against the marriage. She was from another tribe and 'too educated'. When her father's body had been brought back from Nairobi for burial, a makeshift shelter had had to be built to symbolize the house he had never got round to building. Her mother had flatly refused though, to undergo any of the intricate traditional rituals that went with the mourning period and her father's burial. This had made her husband's relatives dislike her even more. Carol was aware that they all said—and probably believed—that her mother's condition was as a result of her refusal to take part in the rituals. And that was the reason why most of their relatives didn't want anything to do with them.

Carol had had to grow up fast and understand such complicated grown-up matters. Sometimes she felt so overwhelmed, tired and worn out that all she wanted to do was lie down and not rise again. But if she did, what would happen to her mother, her brother and her sister? They had no one else to turn to. If she kept going, then at least they could hold on to her and plod on ahead with her.

"Grego!" Carol called out in the direction of her uncle's house. She seldom had to call out twice. She knew her brother would be back in the house in a few minutes. That is how they all obeyed her. She was, after all, the 'man' of the family. She was the breadwinner and symbol of authority. That, and also the mother of the home who had to comfort, cook, clean and care for everyone. It had become natural for her to make sure that the others were fed, clean and alright before she worried about her own personal issues. Technically, to her two siblings—and their mother—she was not only their dad but also their mum, although she was only a child herself.

4

Even when you don't see

Believe it and it is

In everything around us

Against every forbidding wall

Under all dark covers

The hope you need is near

But only if you listen

And even when you don't hear

Listen harder and you will feel.

~Birdsong

The woman they all called 'Birdsong' repeated after the birds as they saluted the arrival of a new day. It was incredible how she made up words that exactly matched the rhythm of the sounds that the birds made;

Slip-slap three!

Slip-slap three!

Slip-slap three!

Free the area! Free the area! Free the area!

For those who had not known her before, it was difficult to believe that she was better educated than most people in the village. She had gone to very good schools in the city and even to the university. Now she was just a madwoman with unkempt hair, dressed in tattered clothes most of the time.

"Come and drink your tea Mum!" Carol wearily called out to her. Greg and Paulette had already had their breakfast- a mug each of watery tea and boiled sweet potatoes. They had already left for school. Carol usually waited until they had all, including their mother, had their food before she ate whatever was left. It was a habit she had slowly developed over the time she was the head of the family.

"I am singing with the birds!" her mother answered her like a stubborn child.

"I can hear you singing with the birds, but I want you to come and take your breakfast right now!" Carol said a bit sharply. Her mother usually obeyed her whenever she talked in that tone. She slowly shuffled into the house with a sulky pout on her face. Carol pointed to the enamel mug on the small coffee table and her mother sat on the stool and slowly cupped the mug in her still shapely hands.

"Are you going to work?" she asked her daughter, who had now walked over to a corner of the house where a broken piece of mirror hung from a nail.

She was slowly brushing back her hair and plaiting it at the nape of her neck.

"To school Mum...I'm going to school! I'm just a kid... your kid!" Carol suddenly found herself yelling at her mother. She could feel angry tears burning the back of her eyelids. But she couldn't tell who or what she was angry at. Perhaps everyone...everything! The fact that her mother thought she was the grown-up, who should make her do everything like a child, or the fact that everything that could possibly go wrong had gone wrong, and now her life was a living nightmare.

She noticed that her mother was looking at her with fear and confusion clearly showing in her eyes and she suddenly felt a twinge of pity and guilt.

"I'm going to school," she said in a gentler tone, "just take your tea." She gently patted her mother's stubbly head. The petite, dark-skinned lady whose figure had remained trim and shapely even after three children had been the envy of the many friends she had had then. Carol remembered how her mother had such luxuriant hair before. It had been so long, it went below her shoulders. That too had been much coveted by every one of her friends. Now it had to be kept very short because her mother in her present condition could never keep it clean and neat.

'Birdsong' stared at her daughter with a quizzical look on her face, which was still quite beautiful by many standards, even now that she was sick. Just as a few years back when she was well, it had been hard to believe that she was 'on the wrong side of forty' and definitely not a spring chicken by any means. She had retained her physical charms and had been aging so gracefully. Her petite frame, captivating wide eyes with slightly brown irises and shapely, even lips on the heart-shaped face that always had a smile on it would easily have made anyone confuse her for someone in her early twenties.

Carol was a perfect replica of her mum physically. A small frown had now formed on her face as if she was trying hard to concentrate and remember who she was and what had happened. The look on her mother's face made Carol so sad. She wanted to sit down beside her, put her arms around her and comfort her, just the way her mother had done for her several years back when she was a child.

This particular morning, Carol had a very bad feeling deep down in her heart. It was as if her intuition was trying to warn her of something, but she brushed the feeling away. In any case, she had to go to school. Mostly, her mother spent the days roaming around the village, talking about the songs the birds sang with anyone who cared to listen to her. A lot of the time she went to the local market, and some of the women would make her do jobs for them like plucking and cutting up vegetables or peeling potatoes, giving her food in return. Carol usually left some food for her in case she felt hungry and came back to the house for something to eat. Once she left in the morning though, she seldom came back to the house. She would come back in the evening and Carol would have no idea where she had been the entire day.

That was what the woman who had been so many students' favorite teacher, who had planned to take evening classes for her master's degree, and had a collection of poetry she had dreamt of getting published, had become. Before she became *Lwa-Manyonyi* – 'Birdsong' – the village madwoman, everyone had known her as Kui. Her real name, however, was Catherine Wangui Ndenga. She had met Carol's father – Chris Ndenga Oyatsi – when she was in her third year of college and he had been a final-year Bachelor of Commerce student. She had been captivated by the quiet, soft-spoken, dark-skinned, muscular hulk of a man with a broad, kind face right from the start, although they did not get married until years after they had graduated from university.

Having grown up and spent most of her life in Nairobi's Eastlands area, tribe was not an issue to her. As a matter of fact she couldn't even speak much of Kikuyu, her parent's ethnic language. She had spoken Sheng, the mixture of English, Kiswahili and forms of several other languages as her 'mother-tongue'. It had been her first language. Her parents had spoken Kikuyu to each other but they always reverted to Kiswahili when speaking to their children. Her late father had owned a small butchery within the estate while her mother had sold used clothes at the famous Gikomba market. They had not made much, but it had been enough to keep their three children in school, food on their table and a roof over their head.

Joshua had not been very good at school, in fact he had often played truant and had to be forced to go to school, but Grace and Kui had been the bright ones— straight 'A' students right from kindergarten. Whatever disappointment their son gave their parents with his alcohol and drugs, the two daughters more than compensated for.

Grace had been high-strung and fun-loving, with a spark of rebellion inside her — and that had been her undoing. This spark deep inside had become a roaring fire by the time she joined the University of Nairobi's School of Law. She always had some cause she was fighting for—the departure of Israelis from the Gaza strip, the introduction of multi-party system ...just about everything. She was at the centre, if not head of, practically every student riot that took place during her time at the college. Before anyone knew about it, she had been thrown out of college, expelled after a couple of suspensions and several warnings. Several salesgirl and modeling jobs later and after the demise of both her parents, she had found herself back in the house she had grown up in, in Ofafa Jericho with three children, each with a different father.

Gracie's squandered life had, to an extent, been the driving force behind her younger sister Kui's success. Kui had been so scared of turning out the way her sister had. She wanted to make something out of her life. Even as she had struggled to develop her teaching career and strived to further her studies, she had always had this whiff of fear, the feeling of 'what if' deep inside her. Perhaps that was why she had taken hefty loans and persuaded her husband to pool it with his own savings and whichever money he cold source elsewhere. He had also taken out a mortgage on his salary just as she had done, after being somehow infected by her enthusiasm. They had finally been able to buy two acres of land in Syokimau, where they had built a one-storey, ten-roomed house with five bedrooms, the two on the upper floor en-suite. She had poured all her feelings and her hopes into this house. It became her very life. It was something very dear and close to her heart, besides her husband and her three children; Caroline, Gregory and Paulette. She had worked very closely with the architect, using the creative streak she had always had to adjust and modify the blueprint they had settled on.

Kui had spent a lot of her life in a cramped two-bedroomed city council house. Her entire family and whichever of her relatives was visiting or living with them as they went to college or looked for a job had to share the confined space. Then when she and Ndenga got married, she had moved into his house in Komarock, which had been more spacious, a palace as far as she was concerned then. She had then started dreaming of a real palatial residence that they would not have to pay rent for each month. Her very own house; and when the house in Syokimau was slowly coming into being, she would joke to her friends that her 'castle in the air' was finally becoming a 'castle on the ground'. She had woven so many dreams around it. It was in itself a dream that she had harboured in her heart of hearts for so many years, a dream that she had seen slowly actualizing.

After around five years of scrimping, saving and self-denial, with her earning almost nothing because most of her salary went towards mortgage repayments, her castle on the ground was finally complete. She had thrown as lavish a housewarming party as she could afford then, as soon as her family had moved in. When her friends and the few relatives had moved around the rooms, fingering the drapes and shades, asking what the colour was that she had painted one of the living room walls, discussing the framed paintings on the walls, she had felt fulfilled. She took great pride when they admired the different shades of color on each wall that blended into and complemented each other. She had mixed the different pastels herself with the help of a professional painter to create just the right shades. Her dream had been complete.

She had insisted on getting new furniture and household appliances that 'went' with her new home. A seven-seater leather sofa set, a massive mahogany sideboard on which their flat-screen LCD television proudly reposed and a wall-to-wall Persian carpet that her colleague's husband had got her from Dubai. She wanted all the furniture in all the rooms to be mahogany. And she had slowly had the furniture made to her specifications by a carpenter she had discovered near Kenyatta market. Every stick of furniture, every painting and picture in the house had had a pleasant story attached to it. They had been personal, priceless treasures, every one of them.

Kui had, with the Syokimau house, been like a bird that had flown over fields and meadows searching for just the right grass and reeds to weave her nest with, and the fluff and moss to pad it. Finally, the bird could sing her heart out for joy with the assurance that her mate, eggs and the young ones in time, would have a cozy home of their own. Sadly, the song had been short-lived.

One day, five short months after the family had moved into the house, bulldozers suddenly appeared and tore the house down. Just like that! It was like when a young boy thoughtlessly tears down a nest that has taken a mother bird so long to weave, without realising or caring about the amount of effort, hope, dreams, love and patience that has gone into making it, or the painful heartbreak and sorrow that its destruction would cause.

It had been so sudden! Kui had woken up at five as she usually did, to beat the usual heavy traffic jam along Mombasa road and be at Sunrise Educational Centre, where she taught, in time for the morning lessons. She usually boarded one of the early buses to town, from where she would connect at the Odeon Cinema *matatu* stage to Parklands where the school was located. The bulldozers had arrived just when she was hurriedly taking her breakfast. She had heard an unusual noise outside and looked out through the living room window just in time to see a 'caterpillar' bulldozer pushing down the gate to the home. At first she thought they were being attacked, especially when she suddenly started hearing loud screams from some of her neighbours all around, and the rumbling sound as the buildings crumbled into rubble – a sound which she did not recognise at first. The cup she had been holding fell and shattered on the tile floor as she looked with wide eyes and mouth at the two bulldozers, approaching closer with every second.

Her husband, who had been taking his bath, came running out of the bathroom with only his bathrobe on. It was he who overcame his initial shock at what was happening and quickly went to get the children out of their beds. Little Paulette started howling with horror. Carol and Gregory, still groggy with sleep, asked a lot of questions all at once. Their father pushed them all, including Kui, out of the house just after the large blade of the bulldozer scraped the front porch. He had pushed them all as far away as possible from the house. It was the sight of her neighbours' houses crumbling under the onslaught of the bulldozers that drove Kui out of her trance. She had started screaming like someone in great pain and begun trying to tear herself from her husband's grasp and run back to her house.

All the children had started screaming with her and clinging to her even as she struggled to get out of Chris' firm grasp. In about thirty minutes, the house, her dreams which had taken five years of saving, scraping and sacrifice, was reduced to rubble. They had not been allowed to move anything out; not one of her children's pairs of jeans, not the pearl necklace her husband had brought her back when he had been to The Maldives, not even one of Chris' expensive suits. Neither one of the colorful goldfish from the aquarium nor a single one of the lovely paintings on the walls was saved. Not one thing. Everything they ever owned was suddenly buried under the rubble of stone and concrete that had been the beautiful house over whose design and construction she and Chris had agonized, discussed and sometimes disagreed. And it all happened in less than one hour.

When Kui had not been able to scream anymore, she had collapsed against her husband's massive chest which was bare under the bathrobe, breathing heavily and totally exhausted. She had not even been able to hear the sniffling and sobbing of her children as they clung to her in their night clothes. She stared through swollen and teary eyes at the rubble that had been her warm cozy nest. She and Chris moved around for the rest of the day like people in a nightmare.

Neither of them even remembered to call their places of work and explain what had happened. She had later learned that footage of her, screaming and trying to wrench herself from her husband's restraining grasp with her children wailing around her, was aired on several television channels that evening. In a matter of minutes, hordes of people had descended onto the rubble that had been stately mansions just a couple of hours ago, looting, scrambling and carrying away whatever they could salvage from the rubble like carrion birds fighting over the carcass of a fallen elephant.

Chris and Kui had given up trying to stop what was happening and concentrated on trying to comfort their children. The two younger ones kept asking many questions that did not even register on their parent's numbed minds. Carol was characteristically mature.

People say first-borns are always mature beyond their years, and she really lived up to this assumption. In fact it was she who talked to the kind lady who let them use a vacant room at the back of her shop at the shopping centre while they figured out what to do, and she was just fourteen then. Chris had later called friends whose numbers he remembered off head from a phone he borrowed. Later on, some of these friends brought them the basics; a coffee table, a few plastic chairs, some of their old clothes to change into, a paraffin stove, a couple of mattresses, blankets and a few household utensils.

When Kui later reflected on the incident, she realised that Chris died inside the very second their castle on the ground came crumbling down. It was just his body—the empty shell that had contained him—that collapsed at his place of work a week later, from where he was rushed to Aga Khan Hospital. By the time Kui found someone to stay with Greg and Paulette as she and Carol rushed to see Chris, his heart had ground to a halt. It had been a 'massive coronary', according to the sad-faced doctor who talked to them in the consultation room. Chris's blood pressure had been higher than it should have been for quite a while, but he had never sought treatment because he had never experienced any symptoms. Or perhaps the symptoms had been there and he had simply ignored them — Chris was never one to complain. Dealing with the sudden demolition had made his blood pressure soar uncontrollably, resulting in the massive coronary failure that killed him. They had not even had the chance to say goodbye.

The bank where Chris worked had taken care of the funeral expenses, but Kui had assumed that whatever benefits they were entitled to from contributions to schemes and Saccos would be swallowed up by what Chris must have owed in terms of the loans he had taken to buy the plot in Syokimau and build their ill-fated mansion. Throughout the blur of activities that followed her husband's demise, Kui had stoically struggled to remain strong for her children. She did not even shed one tear. In fact she thought she would never be able to cry again for the rest of her life after that horrible morning when her house was cruelly demolished.

As she later learned, the land they had purchased had been part of the road reserve set aside by the government for the construction of something called 'the southern bypass', which she had never even heard of before. She had always thought a 'bypass' was a surgical procedure! She couldn't get her mind around it. They had purchased the land from what had looked like a genuine real estate agency. She had done due diligence, done a background check, and everything had looked very straight and legal to her! They even had what looked like a genuine title deed. Perhaps it had all been her fault. Chris had trusted her with the responsibility of checking such details, had she failed him? Maybe she had been hoodwinked, easily swindled because of her naïveté. This was the most overwhelming of the heavy thoughts that ground painfully into her already ravaged emotions during the days that followed.

She had found someone in Ofafa Jericho near her childhood home, Ofafa Maringo, who rented one of the two rooms in her house to her. She moved the children into the small room. Then she found Gregory and Paulette places in the nearby city council school—Dr. Shroff primary school. Life had to go on as well as it could, and the children staying in a school of any kind was part of life going on. The more difficult task had been looking for another school for Carol. It was obvious that she could no longer keep going to St. Bakhita Girls, the exclusive, expensive, girls-only convent school she had been attending. Being the go-getter she was, Carol herself had actually gone and talked to the principal of Hekima high school, the nearest mixed day school, where she had been allowed to join. All that was now in the past, however.

"Are you going to Hekima?" Kui asked her daughter, a deep frown forming on her face as she struggled to remember and focus. Snippets of memories from the past kept rebounding and ricocheting uncontrollably inside her head from time to time. Carol put her arm around her mother a bit tighter.

"No Mum, we left Jericho. We are back in the village... we went to Maragoli, Vihiga. Can you remember?" she gazed hopefully into her mother's agonized face, hoping that she would remember, that she would come back.

"Did Daddy get his annual leave?" Kui asked in a small, uncertain voice.

"No!" Carol almost shouted. "Daddy is...Daddy...," and then she started feeling the sharp sting of tears somewhere behind her eyelids and gave up trying to explain to her mother.

"Please don't go away from the house. I left some food in the hotpot if you get hungry." She hugged her mother's stiff shoulders and rubbed her cheek against hers, but Kui didn't respond.

Carol remembered when she had been younger and would often nestle close to her mother, smelling the sweet, flowery scent of the perfume she always wore then. Now she didn't smell sweet anymore, and she couldn't even remember who she was or what had happened. Carol quickly pulled herself together, nimbly secured her braid with a rubber band and plastic clip, picked up her school bag and left. She still had a small nagging feeling at the back of her mind like a small rat clawing and gnawing away. She tried to keep it out of her mind as she walked briskly along the dusty, untarmacked road that led to Hillside. She was already late. In the bushes along the road, a dove called out plaintively as if talking to her;

Guku! Leta kwiti!

Guku! Leta kwiti!

Guku Leta kwiti!

5

The heart travels

Its own journey

Flirting from tree to tree

Love has its own wing

Beating with its pace

When two beaks touch

Then two hearts become one

Love is a heart with a beat all its own

Love is a breath unlike another drawn.

  ~Birdsong

That the two best chemistry students in her small school had chemistry between them was not something that was lost to the sharp-eyed Madam Juliet. And she did not hesitate to tease them about it in her quiet manner when she talked to them about the upcoming science congress. She needed them to put their heads together and come up with a project for Hillside Academy to present at the event, which was to be held a month from then. That was the reason she summoned them both to her tiny cubicle of an office that morning.

"Come up with, you know, something! I believe you two can come up with more creative things than whatever sweet nothings you must whisper into each other's ears," Madam Juliet smiled cheekily as she said that.

Carol suddenly felt shy and looked at the floor and Saidi laughed nervously. Even Madam Juliet had noticed their close friendship! Had they been that obvious?

"It is okay Caroline, don't be so coy, you are the city girl!"

Carol realised that she was twisting and pressing hard onto the biro pen she was grasping hard in her sweating hand. She couldn't understand why she was so nervous and uneasy.

"I'm looking forward to seeing the child that these two minds put together will produce." Juliet was still smiling warmly and cheekily as she gestured them out of her office. Carol couldn't remember seeing the old woman so cheerful, she was always so tired.

"*Ngai!* Can you imagine that? She is already imagining us with a baby," Saidi muttered as they went back to class.

"She didn't mean that kind of child, idiot! She was talking about a brainchild—an idea—that sort of thing!" Carol responded sharply, her voice rising slightly with irritation.

"But the other child, you know, the one not formed in

the brain will not be a bad idea too, okay not here and now but..." Saidi was grinning cheekily.

"What!" Carol gasped. "Not here, not now, never anywhere else and never any other time, never!"

She controlled her voice as she said that because they were passing by some of the other classes. She felt so shy about what Saidi had said that had she been a few shades lighter, she would have blushed to the roots of her hair. The fact was that the thought of someday being with Saidi and having children together had crossed her mind quite a few times. Okay, she had read and heard that people often married their high school sweethearts...sweetheart? Would she describe Saidi as her 'sweetheart'?

Okay she really liked him, the way he talked, with his voice sometimes cracking as it was yet to complete its transition from a boyish squeak to the deep bass of an adult man. She loved the way his dark hair framed his brown face in curls and wisps, as if he had applied some curling chemical on it, although that was how it was naturally. And he was so funny; he always made her laugh even during the toughest of times.

Whenever she thought about him, her heart beat faster, and whenever things were tough and she the thought of facing yet another day weighed her down, her mood always brightened considerably whenever she thought of meeting Saidi. The mere thought of seeing him again was enough sunshine to drive away clouds, however heavy and dark they may be. But she didn't want to tell that to him openly, and she most certainly didn't want other people to notice.

"A chemistry project is something really appropriate, don't you think? Who would have thought Madam Juliet would have been keen enough to notice the chemistry between us..." Saidi mumbled from the corner of his mouth, only to hiss sharply with pain as she kicked one of his ankles.

She covered her mouth with one hand to stifle the giggle that his spontaneous show of pain brought.

They had arrived at the door of their class, Form Three B, and she quickly entered before he could do or say anything else, and he followed her in closely.

"Did she give you any punishment?" Bella Ukiru, who sat just next to Carol, whispered in an excited manner. It was then that Carol noticed that the entire class was staring at them with looks of silent curiosity.

"Punish us for what?" Carol whispered back.

"For being... you know... caught..." Bella seemed embarrassed by what she was saying.

"Caught!?" Carol was quite puzzled. Bella, realising that she was about to put her foot into her mouth, quickly shrugged and pretended to be rummaging inside her desk for some book.

Then Carol heard Saidi give a barely stifled guffaw at the right back corner of the classroom where his desk was. She turned around sharply, just in time to see a couple of the boys who sat next to Saidi giving him the same weird looks identical to the one that Bella had just given her. She turned to Bella again, grasping her sleeve a tad harder than she intended.

"What is happening?" she asked through clenched teeth.

"Hey...nothing..." Bella tried to pull the sleeve of her pullover out of Carol's grasp.

"It certainly is something, come on tell me...please..." Carol decided to plead.

"Okay, someone said you were caught having...you know...doing it, in a bush near your home, and you got reported to Madam Juliet."

For a moment, Carol stared at Bella unbelievingly.

"What?" she gasped, truly shocked at what she had just heard.

Bella nervously tugged her sleeve out of Carol's grasp, successfully this time and shrugged again.

"One of the boys... I just heard it..." Carol felt so furious that she almost choked on her anger. She stood up and angrily faced the rest of the class.

"Whoever wants to start rumors should be bold enough to face me instead of spreading lies!" her voice choked with emotion. "Saidi and I were summoned by Madam Juliet to discuss a project for the regional science congress! I have never been ..." her words trailed away as she felt the all too familiar sting of tears at the back of her eyelids.

"You don't have to explain yourself to anyone... let people say whatever they want to. So what if we had been doing that?" Saidi said from the back of the class and most of the other students laughed at that.

Carol felt so angry! It was as if Saidi was enjoying all of it. But she was the girl — the one who would feel the shame. The boy would be seen as the hero and the girl the villain, even if both of them engaged in the same act at the same time. That is one of the ways that being a girl sucks. Carol longed to put her head in her arms and cry her heart out.

Luckily, before she could unleash more drama, Miss Sagala clip-clopped into the classroom in her stilettos, the whiff of her strong, musky perfume preceding her into the room by quite a few seconds.

"What is the meeting about?" she asked in her high-pitched voice. Miss Sagala's light-skinned face was framed by one of the silk scarves — *hijab* — which she always wore to cover her hair. The long-sleeved blouse and ankle-length skirt, similar to the others she always wore did not hide at all the fact that she had a very slim, attractive figure. She was quite young, barely in her mid-twenties, and she easily connected with and related to her students.

Everyone clamped up, and those who had been standing or turning around in their seats immediately sat down and faced the front of the classroom.

"Come on, I asked what this 'parliament sitting' is all about, I heard quite some intense debating as I walked in... enhee! Carol! You seemed to be the speaker, let me hear!"

All eyes turned to Carol. She felt this shameful burning from deep inside her. She could feel her tears dangerously close to her eyelids.

"Come on!" Miss Sagala prodded, "out with it, we have some Mathematics to learn you know."

"They...they are spreading lies about...me...and..." to her dismay, Carol's voice broke. She knew the tears would soon follow, and so she struggled to keep them in.

"Who are spreading what lies about you?" Miss Sagala insisted in a gentler tone.

Carol looked at Bella in exasperation... she really hadn't intended to. She just found herself turning to her. She had wanted to explain that she had heard the rumor from Bella, but Miss Sagala seemed to interpret her glance to indicate that it was Bella who was spreading the rumors.

"Bella the beautiful!" Miss Sagala's voice rang out, "Are you the one spreading slander and rumor around?"

"No! It was not me...I just..." Bella, her eyes widening even more, stammered.

"Yes, continue in that vein, at least we are getting somewhere, you just...what?"

Really, Miss Sagala must have missed her calling, Carol thought just then. She would have made a very good detective or policewoman, if her interrogative skills were anything to go by.

"I...I eeerrmmm...I was only telling Carol what I heard people say," Bella struggled to explain.

Carol could clearly smell the reek of sweat from Bella's tense body as the plump girl struggled to vindicate herself from the suspicion that she was the rumor spreader.

"Who were the people and what were they saying?" Miss Sagala insisted mercilessly.

"They...they said that Carol was caught ...doing...you know...with Saidi..." poor Bella stammered on

"I don't know Bella, until you tell me! What were they caught doing?"

Carol could have sworn that she saw a mischievous glitter in Miss Sagala's eyes as if she was trying to keep a straight face. Why on earth was she torturing Bella so much?

"Ee... Umm... they were playing with each other..." some of the other female students giggled or sniggered at that and most of the boys chuckled with amusement.

"Oh, and what game were they playing?" Miss Sagala persisted.

Carol now felt real sorry for Bella, who was twisting the end of her school tie in her fingers, the damp patch under both her armpits spreading by the second. The rest of the class was having the time of their lives, Carol guessed. They were all paying rapt attention, some of them discreetly jabbing each other in the ribs.

"They were having...sex..." Bella said in a low voice as the giggles in the classroom increased.

"Hey, silence in the court...errmm...classroom!" Miss Sagala rapped her table with a wooden ruler.

It was then that it occurred to Carol that the teacher was imagining herself in the judge's seat, presiding over a serious case. Her mood brightened up considerably and she started listening to Miss Sagala with a lot of amused interest. She looked fixedly at the top of her desk to avoid looking straight into Miss Sagala's eyes.

"Oh. And who said that Carol and Saidi were caught having sex?" the teacher continued her interrogation.

"The boys...Nicholas..." Bella blurted out.

"Nicholas is one boy. How many others said it? Were they chorusing it out like a choir?"

"N...no...it was just Nicholas," Bella said, her voice shaking by then.

"Nicholas! Yes! Tell us, when and where did you catch Carol and Saidi you know... being intimate?"

Nicholas Adika was a very talkative short, stocky, cross-eyed boy who was always wisecracking. It sometimes got him into trouble with the other students when he taunted and poked fun at them, but his sturdy, muscular build always made them avoid any physical confrontation with him. It was obvious that he wasn't one that could be easily tackled in a physical fight.

"Heey, Madam, I did not say that!" Nicholas noisily shot up from his seat, his desk loudly scraping the floor in the process.

"Order! Order Nicholas, speak while sitting down!" Miss Sagala rapped the top of her table with her ruler again. "I will not tolerate...that!" Carol bit her lower lip to stifle a smile. She was quite sure that Miss Sagala had been about to say 'such disorderly conduct in my courtroom'.

"Madam, I did not say anything of the sort!" Nicholas continued in his usual loud, scratchy bass voice.

"What did you say then?"

It was obvious that Miss Sagala had forgotten all about the day's Mathematics lesson and was having the time of her life presiding over the impromptu courtroom drama.

"Carol and Saidi had been summoned to Madam Juliet's office... and we...all of us... were just wondering why...Me, I just suggested perhaps they had been caught doing something, you know, bad...like...eerrmm...what Bella said..."

Most of the students laughed out loud at that.

"Order!" the teacher rapped her table once more. "So it was just a wild thought in your head — a figment of your imagination...you had no proof, no basis, and in fact no grounds at all for this allegation?"

Carol was by then looking with a lot of interest into Miss. Sagala's face. Exactly what was the teacher up to? Was it really just a matter of solving the rumor-mongering incident? Carol could not tell just by watching her face.

"So you did not specifically say they had been caught having sex?" Miss Sagala asked when Nicholas did not respond to her first question.

"No! I only said what if they had! Eh?" Nicholas said forcefully, as overconfident as he always was. Miss Sagala turned to poor Bella, who sat hunched up in her chair, looking as if she was about to burst into tears at any moment.

"Bella the beautiful! Is that what you told Carol...or did you warm it up and add some spices and salt of your own?"

Carol suddenly felt very sorry for Bella.

"Uhhm, Madam, I think I overreacted..." she tried to go to her friend's rescue.

"I was speaking to the acc...eerm...to Bella! She surely does have a tongue of her own, doesn't she?" the teacher insisted.

"I'm sorry..." Bella whispered, her voice hardly audible.

"Speak up please Bella... what did you tell Carol exactly?" Miss Sagala mercilessly prodded.

"I...I told her that people were saying she was caught in the maize field with Saidi, and...and Madam Juliet called them to her office... to... to talk to them about it..."

"And you did that knowing too well that it was not true?"

"I...I'm sorry..." Bella drew in a gurgling breath, and a single tear fell from one of her eyes onto the top of her desk.

"Upon your admittance of guilt, your cooperation with this cou.....me, and your show of remorse, I hereby let you off with a strong warning. From now henceforth, don't tell anyone else wrong information that would cause them unnecessary anxiety and distress. And as for you Nicholas, learn to differentiate between figments of your wild imagination, and actual happenings! This case is closed." She tapped her table with the ruler yet again, this time with an obviously amused smile on her face.

"I would have made a splendid judge somewhere... honestly," she said with a sudden ear-to-ear grin, making the entire class burst out laughing, which lightened the tense atmosphere considerably.

"Now! For some Mathematics," her face became serious once more as she drew back the long sleeve of her light blue blouse and glanced at her tiny wristwatch.

"Enough time wasted already, Marvin, clean up the blackboard for me, and the rest of you, take out your 'Advanced Mathematics' and turn to chapter twelve."

Carol heaved a sigh of relief as she rummaged inside her desk for her textbook. Still, the nagging, anxious feeling wouldn't go away from the back of her mind. She somehow knew that the drama of the day was far from over.

6

Hello,

Can't you hear me calling?

Hey!

Don't you see me falling?

Where is the 'we are one'?

Why is your ear blocked to me

Aren't we in the same ocean

Or have we drifted apart?

Is your eye blind to my plight?

Is your route a different flight?

Hello?

Can't you hear me calling

Hey!

Didn't you see me falling?

  ~Birdsong

By the time Carol had finished vacuuming Madam Juliet's small living room, tidied up and arranged the newspapers and books in and on top of the small bookcase near the tiny television set, the sun was drowsily sinking into her cloudy covers where she could close her glowing eye and rest for the day. Carol boiled water for the old lady's evening cup of tea and carefully poured it into the small blue thermos flask that was usually used for the purpose. She then plugged in the small heater and turned it on, with the heat moderate just the way Madam Juliet, who was in the bathroom having her evening shower, liked it.

Carol had already made the mashed potatoes, the way Madam had instructed her to be making them — mashed with some milk and a pat of butter to a smooth consistency, neither too soft nor too hard. She had it ready in a food flask, next to the other food flask that contained some chicken broth she had also warmed earlier. The old lady found cooking tedious and as she had explained to Carol, 'the old hands keep shaking more each day' and she couldn't trust herself with delicate things like cooking or handling the gas cooker. She usually had some cereal and cold milk for breakfast and took something made for her in the school kitchen for lunch. Carol made supper for her after school and left it in the flasks for her after she had cleaned and tidied up the small house.

"Madam, I'm off now!" Carol called out to Madam Juliet after she had picked up her school bag from the coffee table in the sitting room.

"Okay dear, take care." Madam Juliet answered above the sound of the water in the shower.

As she made her way past the now silent school back to the village, the uneasy feeling that had gnawed at her mind all day started getting stronger. As much as she tried to push it out of her mind and dismiss it as just the effect of the 'case' earlier in the day, it kept coming back.

She stopped to buy a few bunches of kale from Tafroza's stall just around the corner from her home. Tafroza was always kind to Carol and her siblings, and often let her have vegetables, onions or tomatoes on credit. The tiny hut in which she and her family lived seemed eerily silent as she drew near. By that time her mother would usually have made her way back and would be singing or putting words to the sounds the birds made at sunset. Or she would be engaging in one of her arguments with little Paulette. Something deep inside her warned her of danger. She quickly walked into the hut and found Paulette sprawled on the mud floor, writing in one of her books. The fading light made her put her face closer to the book than she normally would have, all the better to see whatever she was writing, probably her homework.

"Sasa? Where is Mum?" Carol asked her little sister without waiting for her to return her greeting.

"I don't know. We didn't find her here when we came back," Paulette answered without stopping what she was doing.

"And Grego?" Carol was beginning to get worried, although she didn't quite understand why.

"He is at uncle's," Paulette answered.

"How many times have I told him not to be spending all his time at..." Carol's tirade was cut short just then, when Big Susy burst into the hut without knocking.

"Kaaro!" she gasped breathlessly. She must have walked very fast or run for quite some distance.

"What is it Susy?" Carol's head reeled and she almost swooned. Now she was sure something terrible must have happened to her mother or Greg.

"Kaaro, come with me quickly...your mother..." Susy gasped on, already going outside without waiting to catch her breath. Somehow, Carol found the strength to rush outside behind Susy.

"Wh...what happened...is she..." Carol couldn't bring herself to mouth the fears she had at the time. When she and her mother had their roles switched around by fate, she had started feeling towards her mother exactly the way a mother feels about her small child, including sensing by some inner sixth sense or intuition whenever her mother was in some danger or was not feeling well.

"What happened...where...where is she..." she asked breathlessly as she trotted behind Big Susy.

"We have to take her to the hospital quickly...they did ... very bad things to her..." Carol almost fainted at Big Susy's words. But somehow, she found the strength to keep up with the older woman's surprisingly quick pace. There was no time for further questions. They soon arrived at a section of Majengo shopping centre, where there was a field that used to be part of the local slaughter house before the local authorities had relocated it. A crowd had gathered at the corner of the field. Carol's heart beat faster and faster as they drew nearer to the spot.

Big Susy pushed people out of their way until they reached the centre of the crowd where Carol saw her mother lying still and quiet at the centre. She looked so vulnerable and small, like a sleeping child. Carol quickly dropped to her knees and anxiously looked closer at her mother. She sighed with relief when she noticed that her mother was breathing, although her eyes were tightly closed. At least she was still alive. Her clothes had apparently been ripped off and her face was a little puffed up, as if she had been hit hard. Carol also noticed some drops of blood on the grass around her mother. She noted with a deep sense of gratitude that it was Big Susy's leso that was tied around her mother. Without it, she would have been totally naked.

"We must get her to the hospital quickly," Big Susy, who had dropped down to her knees beside Carol whispered again. Carol's head was spinning and she just couldn't think straight. It was Susy who had to take charge once again and talk to the owner of a motorbike 'taxi', who agreed to carry her mother's limp body, with Carol sitting behind her to support her. The motorbike slowly took them to the health centre, which was not very far away.

* * *

"It is called PEP-post exposure prophylaxis. It is medicine that is taken for a few days by people who may have been exposed to HIV during rape or other unprotected sexual contact, or other ways in which they may have come into contact with the body fluids of infected persons. PEP reduces the chances of contacting the virus that causes AIDS," the pleasant nurse explained to Carol. "She must take one of these pills daily for twenty six days", she continued.

Carol sat motionless in front of the nurse's table. She was exceedingly grateful for Big Susy's support; she just didn't know what she would have done without her. Big Susy had been with her most of the time after the unfortunate incident, only leaving to attend to Greg and Paulette and her own three children the previous evening.

Carol had had to spend the night at the hospital with her mother and had not gone to school that day. She could not imagine what horror her mother had gone through. The doctor had said that besides being raped, she had also been severely beaten, probably when she tried to resist. When she had recovered her consciousness, she had clung to Carol like a frightened child and cried as if she was in great pain. One of the cuts on her face needed a few stitches, but the rest only needed some liniment and a dab of iodine tincture, which Carol was instructed to apply every day to help bring down the bruises. Carol knew that the bandage that had been put onto her mother's right forearm would not last for long after she became fully conscious. She was surely going to tear it off. Huddled quietly in the seat next to her, Carol's mother was obviously still bewildered and in pain.

"How do we make her take the medicine sister?" Big Susy asked the nurse, "She is the way she is you know… it is not easy."

Carol looked at her friend again with that feeling of gratitude. She noted that Susy had always said 'we' and 'us' since the previous evening when it all happened. She had seen it as much her problem as it was Carol's. None of Carol's relatives had turned up at the hospital to enquire after their welfare, but Big Susy had been there all the time. Carol felt the tears welling up in her eyes and fought them back. What would she have done without Susy?

"It is okay to carefully crush the pill and put it in a cold glass of milk or fruit juice," the nurse told them.

After they had returned to the small hut, Susy had helped Carol take her mother inside before going to attend to her own chores. It was only then that Carol began thinking about school. There was the chemistry project she had to think about, the continuous assessment tests were coming up… and Madam Juliet needed her to go and do the chores for her in the evening. There was so much to think about. The nurses at the hospital had asked her to report the incident at the local police station so she could be given a p3 form, but Carol was too overwhelmed. It had been a daunting task calming down her mother when she had regained consciousness during the night, and she hadn't slept for a single second.

She fluffed up the old mattress on the only bed they had in the house, and straightened the single sheet and the threadbare blanket over it before gently helping her mother to lie down on it. She then unfolded the mattress that Gregory and Paulette usually shared and stretched herself on it. She was fast asleep almost before her head hit the mattress.

* * *

Big Susy's footsteps woke her up late into the afternoon.

"Oh, were you asleep?" Susy asked without really needing an answer. She glanced into the other room where Carol's mother was lying on the bed and staring at the roof of the hut.

"How is she?" Susy asked, her hoarse voice fading into a whisper.

"Well...," Carol shrugged her shoulders,

"You will need to report this *kifwaavi*, this mess to the police." Susy patted Carol's shoulder lightly. "They write for you something called *piizuri* then the doctor signs it. Jemsi was given one of those when his brother cut him on the head with a panga after they had words over the piece of land!"

Susy started bubbling excitedly in her usual manner. Carol wanted her to continue talking, even if she was not particularly listening. Susy was technically her best friend now, despite the age difference between them and the fact that

Big Susy was illiterate and from a different planet, so to speak. There was Bella Ukiru, Saidi and of course Madam Juliet, but she related to them differently. She could tell Susy anything, and Susy was always there to help in ways that none of the rest could. Carol had by now learned most of the local language – her father's language – which people talked most of the time in the village, apart from Susy. Before she had had to live in the village, she had not known more than just the few words which she had learned from her father.

"It is no use going to the police station...she will recover," Carol shrugged her shoulders wearily. She had come to associate the police with unpleasant feelings. The people who had demolished their house in Syokimau had been accompanied by scores of armed policemen, who had not done anything to prevent the looting that had taken place after their house and those of her neighbours were demolished.

"No... it is a good thing to do so... besides the people who did this are known. It was that rascal, Bunyoli and his friends, they should be arrested." Susy grabbed Carol's shoulder as she said that.

"It may only cause more trouble for us. People you know...don't like us a lot around here. If we send someone to jail, they will only hate us more." Carol hunched up her shoulders, and she must have looked very pathetic because Big Susy stopped her gushing and put one of her plump arms around her shoulders.

"I see what you mean. Just leave them to God. They will get the payment for what they did right here on this earth."

Both started and looked into the other room as the bed creaked noisily when Carol's mother tried to get up.

"I want to go outside, I need to pee," she said in a weak voice, much like a child. Carol hurried over to help her up and support her to the back of the hut. She was relieved to hear her speak. Deep inside, she had been so afraid that she would revert to silently staring at the roof and wetting her bed as she had done when she first became ill. Even thinking about those worry-filled days made Carol start to get that hollow, empty feeling she was now all too familiar with. During those days, she had sat by her mother's bedside, waiting and hoping and wishing so hard that she would recover and get up from the hospital bed. She was not used to making decisions and she had needed her mother. She had been barely fourteen! All she had wanted was for her mum to come back home and take care of everyone as she had always done.

With time, Carol had learned the tough truth, that her mother was not going to be able to take care of anyone else, and in fact, she was also going to need to be taken care of. Just a child then, she had quickly learned that people could only be generous to a certain extent, after which they started seeing you as a bother.

The owner of the tiny room in Ofafa Maringo wanted her rent every month, regardless of how they got it or whether her mum was sick and they were having problems. The money they had got from selling her dad's Toyota Corolla—at a desperate throw-away price—was gone after some time. After they had failed to pay rent for about three months, their landlady had started asking them to move out.

It had been such a nasty part of her life. Her mother had just lain on the bed in the corner of the room staring at the roof and not speaking a single word. Auntie Gracie usually brought them food and tried to talk to her mum and make her talk, but she never did. It had been quite clear even then to Carol that Auntie Gracie couldn't be relied on to help any longer, and the number of people they could turn to for help were decreasing each minute. So she decided that the only place they could go was to her late father's home village-Igina, in Maragoli.

She had gone to her mother's former place of work— the school at which she used to teach—and after sitting on the bench outside the principal's office for hours trying to gather the courage, she finally asked the secretary to allow her in. It had been the principal who gave her the money she bought the bus tickets with.

The journey back home had been a nightmare, with her mother soiling herself in the bus much to the chagrin of the other travelers. And it had been a worse nightmare for her to adjust to life in the village and to take care of everyone else. But now she was used to it, besides, the village air had revived her mother somehow. Although she had lost all memory of who and what she was, at least she could walk around the village and talk once more, even if none of what she said made any sense. The doctor at the hospital had said that if she got the treatment and therapy she needed, Carol's mother could recover fully with time.

"Careful...." Big Susy said as she helped Carol ease her mother back onto the bed.

"Mama Chantal?" Carol's mother asked in a small, bewildered voice as she looked at Big Susy with the puzzled frown that always appeared on her face whenever she was trying to figure out something, or when lost memories tugged at her, trying to flow back into her troubled mind.

"No Mum," Carol couldn't help smiling as she leaned over her mother. "This is not Mama Chantal, it's Susy! We are no longer in Nairobi."

Mama Chantal had been their neighbor in Syokimau, and her house had also been destroyed. She had been as round and roly-poly as Big Susy.

"She is confusing you with her friend back in Nairobi who... uhmm...looked a bit like you," Carol explained to Big Susy. Her friend laughed her hoarse chesty laugh, holding one of her pudgy hands to her face.

"*Magu*! You mean there is someone who actually looks like me in Nairobi? With a face as ugly as mine?" But she was obviously flattered.

Carol's attention had wandered back to her mother; she always hoped that her mum would somehow start remembering things once more whenever she seemed to be straining to recall.

"Mum? Are you feeling any pain?" she asked.

"No...no..." the frown and look of concentration remained firmly on her mother's face.

"Bad men.... Hurt me...," tears welled up in her eyes as she said it and Carol put her arm around her stooped shoulders.

"You will be fine...You will be fine Mum," she assured her, swabbing at the single tear that oozed from the corner of one of her eyes and slowly made its way down her cheek.

"Has she eaten anything?" Big Susy asked. Trust her to think about food and eating even at the most inappropriate times!

"No, I haven't had the time to prepare any food yet."

Susy turned around and picked up a polythene bag she had brought along.

"I brought some maize and beans."

She took out a large plastic bowl with a lid. There was a time when Carol would eat *githeri* only when the maize and beans were fried, with a lot of spices, meat, potatoes and carrot and some other accompaniment. But as things were at the moment, anything that could take the edge off the constant hunger pangs was very welcome. She looked at Big Susy with a lot of gratitude as she took the plastic bowl from her. It was so amazing that someone with so little herself was ever ready to share that with others. Even the time she was taking to visit and sit for a while with Carol and her mother was a sacrifice. She would ordinarily be doing some casual job on someone's farm or doing household chores for the money she needed so much to feed her three children at such a time.

"It's only a little, but what can one do? Just make do with it." Big Susy shrugged her shoulders.

"A little?" Carol laughed a little with surprise, "This is enough for all of us...even Grego and Paulette; I will keep some for them."

She was very grateful. There had been no food in the house.

"I wonder if you will be able to leave her alone in the house tomorrow. There will be work at Mzee Manoah's, his son will be completing that building he started last month." The next day was a Saturday; the day Carol usually did casual jobs for extra money.

"Building? *Mjengo*?" she was a bit amused. What she and Big Susy usually did was farm work or household chores – laundry and housecleaning and such jobs. She had always assumed that construction site jobs and other heavy menial jobs were for men and boys.

"Yes! These days you do whatever can bring some coins into the pocket!" Big Susy told her, patting her rather too hard on the shoulder with a plump hand.

"Do women do that?" Carol looked at Susy with a doubtful scowl.

Big Susy chuckled and patted her shoulder again. "There usually are more women than men. Even Kadesa will be coming, to make money for her man to get drunk with." Big Susy's face scrunched up into a disapproving and knowing pout, her voice lowering to a hoarse, conniving whisper that was still quite audible for a few hundred metres around.

"What?" was all that came out of Carol's mouth. A lot of things crossed her mind as she listened to Big Susy.

"Yes, her man demands most of the money she earns from these *vibarua-vibarua*, casual jobs, to drink with and buy cigarettes, if she ever refuses he beats her very thoroughly!"

In spite of herself, Carol felt very sorry for the woman who had always been unkind to her. Perhaps it was all that she was going through that made her so bitter and hateful! Carol had seen Magwaro, Kadesa's husband, from a distance a couple of times, but this was the first time she was hearing that.

"But what kind of man does that? Aren't men supposed to work and support their wives and children?" she asked with genuine surprise.

"*Baya*! I tell you! They say my Jemsi didn't go to school, but he sends me whatever he makes in Nairobi, and I have to work to earn something more to add to it, so that the children and I can live, but some men are just not men at all! Kadesa's man was a teacher, but what did he do? He drank and drank until everything he ever learned in school was wiped off his brain by the alcohol! And now she has to give him money to drink and buy cigarettes with. And I am asking you Kaaro, will a woman know what the children will eat or how a grown-up man will drink *chang'aa*?"

Big Susy shrugged her shoulders. Carol was astounded by what she had heard. She had been raised to believe that men were responsible, the way she remembered her father had been. He had always put the interests of his family before his own. Even at that very young age, Carol had fully realised that. She remembered very well the affection with which her father always treated her mother. If they had ever had any problem, their children never saw it. He certainly would never have beaten her for any reason.

"*Haya*! You pass by my place tomorrow so that we can go for the job," Big Susy told her as she put the now-empty plastic bowl back into the polythene bag, stood up and shook out her voluminous skirts. Carol felt so much better after her friend had left. She had really needed someone to talk to. And what she had learned about Kadesa was comforting in a way. Now whenever the woman treated her so badly, she would understand what her problem was. She could react with the same patience that Big Susy always did whenever Kadesa treated her shabbily.

Carol picked up the tiny battered black and grey 'Cony' radio, whose manufacturer had obviously intended to take advantage of the more popular 'Sony' brand. The 'on' dial gave a sharp click as she turned it on, but the radio made no other sound. She gave it a few sharp slaps and a vigorous shaking and it cackled, coughed, gasped and came to life. The hissing sound of static interfered with the music playing on Zic FM, her favorite station but she was used to that now. This was not the home theatre system with wireless speakers placed at different positions around the living room of the house in Syokimau. That life was gone and it was no use thinking about it now. She took a plastic jug and drew some water from an old black container branded 'Skyplast' and sprinkled it on the dusty floor of the hut. She then swept the floor with a broom made from reeds tied together with a strip of elastic rubber.

She needed to get some cow dung to mix with ash and clay to plaster the floor with. She usually got that from her uncle's place, or Big Susy's. That was one of the things she had gotten used to with time. At first, she had been petrified at the thought of even touching cow poop, but now she handled it with ease, without even wrinkling her nose once.

She had learned the hard way that if she didn't keep the floor plastered with cow dung, it would become dusty and attract jigger fleas. All of their feet had been infested with jiggers just a month after they had come to the village before she learned to take that precaution. It had been so painful. But the most painful part had been digging out the bloated little bodies of the troublesome insects with a sewing needle from Greg and Paulette's feet. Her mother had not had a problem with that. She had still been lying silently and passively in bed all day and night then, showing no reaction at all to anything that happened to and around her. The kids though, had screamed their heads off whenever she tried to dig out the jiggers from their toes and soles. Susy had been of great help to her even then— and they had not even been as close as they had become now. She was like an angel, okay, more a roly-poly cherubim perhaps, that God sent to help Carol and her family in that dark period of their lives.

Carol remembered how she and Greg had made a fuss about the type of tiles they wanted on the floors of their rooms in the Syokimau house; tiles that had been imported especially from Dubai at their mother's request. She had listened with amusement as her parents argued and debated over which tiles to use in the living room and the visitors' parlour. Her mum had downloaded heaps of pictures from the internet and spent hours figuring out exactly what she wanted and how she wanted it. And all that had been reduced to nothing in less than an hour.

Carol finished sweeping the two rooms, raising her mum's feet from the floor to make way. She hoped her mum would be fine while she went to Madam Juliet's to do her usual chores. The old lady needed her to go too, whatever the situation was, and she understood this quite well.

Some things in life, one learns by living them, rather than being told. The world is like one large school with classrooms, lessons to learn and teachers everywhere you care to look. Most of these lessons one has to figure out for themselves and the teachers become your teachers only when you accept to learn from them. One vital lesson Carol had learned was that however little you have already, it is a very fulfilling experience to share, even if all you have is a little time to spare.

With her daughter Lindsey away in Canada, Madam Juliet was very lonely and sometimes just needed someone to listen as she talked. Carol realized that she was that person a lot of the time. Madam Juliet was not a very sociable person and she did not have a lot of friends as such. A lot of people who talked to her were those who needed help and saw her as the solution to their problems. Even the holiest of angels must get tired of being looked up to, Carol reasoned. She noticed how cheerful Madam Juliet became while talking to her, whenever she went to clean and prepare her simple meals after school. And she refrained from talking to the kindly old lady about the many problems she and her family went through. She wanted to provide the warmth of companionship, because that was what she had instinctively learned that the old lady needed.

Big Susy had taught her this lesson about sharing—not by preaching it—but by living it. Big Susy seemed to like sharing whatever she had, however small or irrelevant, without even first asking if the person she was giving it to needed it. It was her way of helping. She gave whatever she had to give at that moment, and so often that it had become a sort of reflex.

7

In lows that no wings can surpass

But you are there

And my spirits soar

You are here by my side

You are the lift that I need

Beyond the down

that no wing can lift me beyond.

But here you are

And all is well.

~Birdsong

Saidi seemed unusually pensive and thoughtful that Monday morning. Carol had never seen him being anything else other than playful and full of jokes even during lessons. She was not in the best of moods herself though. It had been quite a weekend. Working at the construction site had been all that she had imagined it would be... and much more. She, together with Big Susy, Kadesa and two other women had started off carrying mortar from where it was being mixed in metal *karais* on their heads and piling it closer to where the mason and his assistants were working on one of the walls. Then one of the boys who had been ferrying bricks from where they had been stacked, slipped and sprained his ankle. Obindi, the man who was in charge of the work, decided that Carol should take over the boy's role.

"The other women are enough to carry the mortar for the *fundi*, you are the youngest and strongest of them," he explained. Kadesa had laughed with so much satisfaction at that. Big Susy had volunteered to do the job but the man had brushed her off.

"You are too fat and slow, let the Nairobi girl do it."

Carol had sensed something cruelly deliberate in the man's voice as he had said that, but she was in no position to argue. Obindi was someone she knew very well—she had turned down his outrageous request for a romantic relationship a couple of months before. In fact, had Big Susy told her that it was Obindi who was the overseer at the site, she would never have agreed to work there. But maybe she would have gone just the same. She badly needed some extra cash. She knew that the time of the month when she needed to buy some sanitary towels was around the corner. The previous month had been pure hell; she had not been able to spare any money for the towels and she had had to bundle together some rags and pad her panties with them since she was doing the midterm continuous assessment tests that she couldn't miss.

She didn't want to get into another nasty confrontation with Obindi— she couldn't afford to—literally. And so she had spent most of the day piling bricks onto the wheelbarrow and struggling to push it to the site. Obindi watched her like a hawk most of the time, making sure she didn't get a moment's rest. By the time they could take a break and have a bite, her whole body was aching horribly and she was on the verge of tears.

"This is life Carol, what can we do?" Big Susy comforted her as usual. "You have to be strong...here, have some of this." She had split the thin *chapatti* she was eating in half and given it to her. They had taken food –githeri and thin, transparent chapattis– from a woman vendor who had brought it over in plastic pails on a wheelbarrow. They would pay her as soon as Obindi paid them for the day. Carol had stared tearfully at the plate of githeri in her hands.

"He just wants to make me suffer," she murmured.

"Why would he want to make you suffer? This is not Nairobi where you can sit around on your behind and live in luxury!" Kadesa had said in her usual arrogant voice.

Carol looked at Kadesa's thin, angry face. She felt a rush of hatred for the woman. Why was she always so cruel? What had she ever done to her? All she wanted was to say something hurtful back to Kadesa. Then she noticed what looked like welts on one of Kadesa's thin cheeks...as if someone had slapped her hard not very long ago. There was also a raw-looking pale spot at the corner of her mouth where she had probably removed the scab over a healing wound.

Suddenly, all the anger that had flooded Carol's heart faded away. She remembered what Big Susy had said about Kadesa and how her husband treated her. Perhaps that was the woman's way of expressing the hurt she felt and the pain she had to go through. And so, instead of saying all the things that had sprung onto her tongue, she just clicked her tongue and turned back to her food.

"Is it me you are clicking your tongue at, you little idiot?" Kadesa had asked angrily, but Big Susy had stopped her before she could say more.

"Kadesa! Listen to me, this child is not your age. Please, let us save our strength for this work, saying a lot of things won't help us in any way." Strangely enough, Kadesa had obeyed her.

It had been one of the worst days Carol had spent, ever! And that was quite something, seeing as she had seen her fair share of bad days in the short span of time since their eviction from Syokimau. She had watched the other women walking with the karais of mortar on their heads, back and forth, over and over again. At some point, one of the women, Nenzi, had taken the shovel from one of the men mixing the mortar and proceeded to do the job just as well as the man had done... if not better.

"A woman can do everything a man does!" Nenzi had responded to the other women's cheerful teasing, "except what the good Lord said should be done only by the men...."

This provoked more laughter and lewd remarks from the other grown-ups. Carol wasn't sure that she should be hearing some of the things that the grown-ups were talking about. That she, only a child, should be doing such tough menial jobs among adults. What struck Carol was the fact that the women were working to feed their families, and the likes of Kadesa to even support their husbands' drinking habits! Something was wrong somewhere, she thought. The day had ended quite dramatically too. Just after all of them had resumed work after their lunch break, Kadesa's husband had staggered to the site, obviously dead drunk.

"Hey! You! Come here!" he had drunkenly called out. It had been very obvious who he had been talking to. Kadesa became visibly agitated and worried-looking.

"Go away Magwaro, we are working!" Obindi had said in a gruff voice.

"I'm talking to my wife...if you want me to marry you too, just say so!" Magwaro's voice grew louder. One of the women giggled.

"If you are looking for a beating, then you have come to the right person," Obindi had growled, his face setting into a mask of anger.

"Just let him be," Kadesa said in a low voice. Carol had never seen her so timid and worried-looking. Kadesa had always been extremely abrasive and arrogant towards her!

"Are these the other men you come and spend your time with in the name of working?" the now very loud Magwaro asked angrily.

Obindi had clenched his fists and started moving towards the drunk man, but the women excitedly dissuaded him from doing anything violent.

"Listen Baba Emma," Big Susy, in her usual peacemaker role, had implored Obindi. "You know how it is...are you equals with him? Don't let him get blood on your hands for nothing."

"Please do you have something, anything I can give him so that he can go away?" Kadesa had whispered urgently. Obindi had hesitated momentarily before handing her a crumpled fifty-shilling note, which Kadesa timidly took to her ranting husband.

"We have not been paid yet, we are still working," she had pleaded fearfully in a whiny voice that Carol had never heard come from her before as she handed over the money to Magwaro.

"You will find me at home. Is this what you do? Taking money from other men?" Magwaro had shouted with his drunken drawl before grabbing the money from Kadesa and staggering away, all the while hurling dirty insults and swearwords. Carol had been petrified. That was something she had never imagined could happen. What was wrong with the man? She had felt so sorry for Kadesa then, in spite of everything she had ever said or done to her before. She had wanted to discuss that with Saidi that Monday at school because she was sure Saidi knew more about Kadesa and her husband. But now it seemed Saidi had weightier issues of his own.

* * *

"Did you eat boiled pepper and raw lemons for breakfast?" Carol asked Saidi as they walked together out of the classroom for the ten o'clock recess. She looked at him with genuine concern when, instead of responding with the usual carefree guffaw, he actually sighed wearily.

"Life's ups and downs," he answered her in an unusually low tone.

"I thought it was all ups with your life."

"Yeaahh, I thought so too," Saidi shrugged his shoulders.

This was one situation that Carol could not think how to deal with. What she was used to was having to take Saidi down a few pegs from time to time. This new Saidi, whose spirits, as it seemed, she would have to prop up was a completely new creature. She waited until they had taken their mugs of porridge from the makeshift school kitchen and settled in their usual corner of the tiny school yard before she broke the silence again.

"Enhe! Tell me now, did they arrange a bride for you or something?" she made another attempt at cheerful teasing, which was met by another deep sigh from Saidi. They had often joked about the fact that Saidi's grandfather thought he should get married and have children instead of going to school.

"I wish it was that simple and pleasant," he smiled at her in a worn, tired manner, perhaps trying hard to regain his usual cheerful self.

Carol smiled encouragingly.

"What is it then?" she kept on prodding.

"They want me to leave school," Saidi winced as if he had felt some pain. Carol couldn't imagine what it was that had eaten into Saidi's confidence like that. And he seemed so shaken and scared that he was obviously finding it difficult to confide even in Carol.

"Saidi..."

All thoughts of her horribly aching body and bruised ego from the weekend's job were forgotten as concern for Saidi preoccupied Carol's mind.

"Please don't talk about this," Saidi said in a low voice.

They were sitting a little further away from the rest of the students, and fortunately, Bella Ukiru no longer tagged after them, after the ridiculous courtroom session with Miss Sagala. Despite all that, Saidi kept looking around with obvious fear in his eyes.

"You know you can tell me anything," Carol assured him in a low voice.

"I... I have been selected along with some other boys to go and be..." Saidi's voice cracked and faded away again.

"To be what, Saidi?" Carol was now very alarmed. She could feel that something was terribly wrong.

"Mujahideen."

Saidi flinched and looked around fearfully after he finally managed to get the word out. Carol noticed a few beads of sweat on Saidi's brow, as if he was scared of even mentioning the word. She had heard that word before, but she couldn't remember, just then, what it really meant.

"What is that?" she asked without really expecting an answer.

"Fighters. I'm supposed to join others fighting for...for the religion." Saidi valiantly struggled to get out the words that obviously struck so much fear into his heart.

Now the picture became clearer to Carol. She had heard about Al-Qaeda, Al-Shabaab, about Boko-Haram... people who claimed to be fighting for Islam and God. She could feel fear closing around her heart like an ice-cold palm. She shivered a little, even though it was quite a hot day.

"Wha...what?"

She hoped he was joking, but it was clear from the expression on his face that he definitely was not. He shrugged his shoulders again. In tortured semi-sentences, the story gradually came out. Saidi's cousin—Mustafa—was in cahoots with some other people who were recruiting Muslim boys from all over Kenya. They would send the boys across the border into Somalia to fight what they called 'the Holy war'. Mustafa had been fiercely opposed to the idea of Saidi going back to school. He had insisted that Saidi could recite and read from the Holy Scriptures, and sing Qasida, and that was all the education he needed, plus the fact that he had been to school up to Class Eight and could read and write. He had wanted Saidi to be taught more of the religious scriptures so that he could become a 'Malaam'— a Muslim scholar.

Mustafa was several years older than Saidi and the son of a brother of Saidi's late father. He owned several businesses around the county and was rich by many standards; he was considered the head of the small Muslim community of 'Mjini'. Mustafa used his father's influence to lord it over the younger members of his extended family and the community. He was their self-declared leader and he expected all that he said to be obeyed.

"I don't understand why you can't just say no! You said you want to go to university, not to go and kill people!" Carol blurted out.

All that she knew about the fundamentalist groups was that they kidnapped and killed people, blew up houses and vented terror on innocent people. She felt a sense of panic, just as if she was the one faced by the hard decision Saidi had to make.

"I... I can't... how do I...?" Saidi's voice broke as he tried to explain that there was just no way that he could go against Mustafa's instructions. Besides, Mustafa worked with other mysterious, dangerous people that no one had seen or knew much about.

Suddenly, Carol felt a surge of anger. She could sense—with that special connection she had developed with Saidi—that he was wishing for a way out of the impasse. He wanted an answer but was scared to even ask. It was not the life he had always dreamt of. Why did some people think they could go around wrecking other people's lives, shattering their dreams? It was so unfair!

"What if I go and face this cousin of yours and tell him you don't want to do this?" she asked.

She said this with a confidence she had developed over the months that she had had to look out for other people beside herself. The same way she went and talked to the parent of the little girl who had been bullying Paulette at school, and the way she had forced one of her cousins to give Gregory back the polythene bag ball he had taken from him. That was the same way she now felt for Saidi. She was going to face Mustafa and threaten to expose him and his network to the authorities if he did not leave Saidi alone. Saidi was horrified to hear that, especially since he knew that Carol was quite capable of doing exactly what she was threatening to do.

"Hey...no!" he almost cried out. The horror on his face was clear and alarming.

"You don't understand. If you do that, you will only be putting yourself into great danger and maybe your family too, not to speak of me," he pleaded.

"Then what do we do? Nothing, just nothing? Will you be going to join these people then?" Carol asked in despair.

"I don't know... perhaps I don't have a choice in this..."

Saidi seemed to shrink into himself as he said this. His very voice had shrunk, from the deep, occasionally breaking bass to a low, quiet whisper.

Carol looked at the ground as if searching for an answer down there somewhere. And strangely enough, she did find one. Right down there! What she saw was a couple of ants struggling with a crumb of *mandazi*, the small buns that were sold at a kiosk across the road from the school, which most of the students bought to take with their mid-morning porridge. The crumb was about three times larger than either of the ants, yet the ants valiantly struggled to carry it, probably to their hole or anthill somewhere. It seemed like a futile thing to try, but that did not deter the two tiny creatures. They had to get food back to their lair or they and others would go hungry.

Suddenly, in some strange way they communicated, the two ants suddenly positioned themselves on one side of the crumb and started tugging with their mandibles towards the same direction. Previously, they had each been pulling in opposite directions. But in their tiny heads, with brains that were probably not visible to the naked eyes, the little creatures had figured out a way around their problems.

Carol had learned from the period after they had been evicted from Syokimau that it was no use merely sitting around and looking at the problem in front of you. It was much better to spend that time figuring out a way around it. There was always a way around every problem. The trick was to figure out in which direction to pull.

"Saidi," she said thoughtfully, tapping her knee with her now empty melamine mug.

"What? You get scary when you think, you know!"

For a moment, Saidi's usual cheeky grin spread across his previously worried face. Carol chuckled a little, glad to see him grin, even if it was for just a few seconds.

"What if someone far away, whom Mustafa can't figure out, helps?"

"Now you are getting scarier. Look, don't let it become your problem okay? This is something you don't understand. Let me just deal with it."

Saidi's shoulders folded up once more. Just looking at him convinced Carol that it was her problem too. He didn't know how he was going to 'deal with it', whatever it was. Carol could sense that her friend was scared. He certainly didn't want to do what he was being forced to. He had his own life, dreams and a future to look forward to. She knew she was the only one who could get him out of the situation.

Thinking about it made her forget everything about Kadesa and her drunken husband, and her mother's rape incident the previous week. Saidi had not even asked her about that, which was evidence that what he was facing was quite grievous indeed. But now she knew what she could do. It was no use just sitting down and sighing over and over about a problem. One has to look for a solution. Every tunnel has to have an end somewhere. The trick was to figure out the way to that opening.

8

Catch the wind, spread your wings

Make the world wide

The den of your hearth.

Drift along, and discover

Ride on your dream

Vanquish and conquer.

~Birdsong

Selkirk Terrace in Duncan on Vancouver Island is the quiet place that Ondisa Chabuga-Walcott had always wanted to live in. Although many people saw it as a retirement community full of senior citizens, it had that quiet tranquility that Ondisa needed for her writing and painting. Apple Bay School was just a couple of blocks away from her house, and sometimes the cheerful, sunny young voices of the students carried over quite clearly. She had finally decided to be true to her lifelong dream and concentrate on her artistic career. Her husband Bruce, who had been her college love, was ready to give her all the support she needed.

When she had been younger, Ondisa had really wanted to marry an African, a Kenyan and preferably a Maragoli like her father. She had always clung fiercely to her African heritage although, frankly, she was bits and pieces of a whole lot of things. Her father's ethnic Maragoli community had been part of the ancient Bunyoro-Kitara kingdom of present-day Uganda before they broke away and migrated into what is now Kenya.

Sadly, because the people hadn't learned writing skills then, a lot of the community's history and heritage had been lost over the years of being passed on orally from generation to generation. Now no one really knew who these people mingled their blood with, conquered and came into contact with over the years. Ondisa knew for a fact that although she was Maragoli on her father's side, she could actually be a mixture of several other ethnic African communities that her ancestors on that side conquered in battle, intermarried with and absorbed along the route to their present home.

Her mother Juliet's Canadian side was even more complicated. Juliet Spencer, as she had been known before her marriage, had been born right there in Vancouver. Her parents could trace their bloodline way back to the first English-speaking people who settled in Canada in the seventeenth century. Before that, Canada had been mostly French-right from 1534 when Jacques Cartier had taken Canada for France. Ondisa took keen interest in her dual heritage. Just as on her father's side, there was an indication that her mother's lineage was also a mixture of several heritages. There was a hint of

French from the ancient past, and it was rumoured that there was some Eskimo Inuit blood in the family as well.

It really excited Ondisa to think that she was a mixture of so many things. The blood of so many people from different worlds flowed in her veins, and those of her twin sons Eddie and Wyatt, whose father had his roots in the highlands of Scotland. If their identical ash-blond shocks of hair and fair complexions were anything to go by, they would certainly have a tough time convincing anyone at all that they could trace their roots to the Bunyoro-Kitara Kingdom of ancient Africa, and that they also had Inuit blood, a few drops of French blood and ancestors who played the bagpipes and wore kilts in the Scottish highlands.

The entire world was connected in one way or another. This is what makes racism, tribalism and all sorts of bigotry so senseless and unnecessary. In a way, we all have a bit of each other in us. Ondisa thought about the official coat of arms of her mother's—now her own—country. The Arms of Canada has been designed such that it reflects the royal symbols of the United Kingdom and France, that is the Irish harp of Tara, the fleurs-de-lis of France, the three lions of England, the lion of Scotland, and a sprig of three Canadian maple leaves to represent the rest of the Canadians. Everyone had been thought of and included.

Her mother had always called her Lindsey after her own mother, but to her late father she had always been Ondisa. Ondisa was also the name of his own mother — her paternal grandmother whom she had never met. Her mother had grown attached to her adopted community in western Kenya; so much that even now that she was quite old and not in very good health, she flatly refused to go back to Canada where she could get better medical care.

Ondisa's brow set in a frown as she remembered the conversation she and her mother had had the previous evening. Something had to be done about the young boy from her mother's school who needed to be rescued from a relative that was trying to recruit him into a terrorist group. She had heard a lot about how the youth were being radicalized and sent to fight wars they did not even understand, but she had always thought that it only happened along the Kenyan coast and the North-eastern part of Kenya where there were large populations of Muslim faithful.

Ondisa picked up the small note book in which she had written the details of her mother's student. Saidi Onzere Salim...hmm. She tapped the book with her pen. Time was essential. Something had to be done very fast. She knew exactly what she was going to do. She was going to get in touch with the press secretary at the Canadian embassy in Kenya. They had met a couple of times when she visited Kenya and they had skyped and emailed each other from time to time. The boy had a good chance of getting asylum in Canada, if only it could be proved that his life was indeed in danger. Alternatively, he could be enrolled in a boarding school in another part of Kenya. Ondisa thought also of the girl that her mother was always talking about. Pauline? No...

Caroline...Yes, Caroline. The girl who, if all that her mother said was true, was quite something. Ondisa had done most of her schooling in an expensive private boarding school at her mother's insistence, but she had spent most of her holidays at her mother's small house in the village. She knew exactly what the village girls went through. They had to do most of the household chores before and after school, and even then the boys were valued more and treated better than them. One of Ondisa's plans was to start a foundation to help such girls and enable them to achieve whatever they set their eyes on. And this Caroline, the apple of her mother's eye, seemed like a very good one to start with.

* * *

"Lindsey will look into it my dear," Juliet said in her soft, slow voice. "I, you know, talked to her last evening after you left."

Carol felt relief surging through her as she heard that. She closed her eyes for a few seconds and exhaled deeply. Saidi's problem had been weighing so heavily on her shoulders. Her reaction did not escape the still sharp, though rheumy, eyes of Madam Juliet. She smiled her cheeky, knowing smile.

"You really love him don't you?" she asked.

Carol cast her eyes aside, too shy to look at her teacher and employer straight in the face.

"Come on! It's nothing to be ashamed of dear, at your age it is bound to happen."

Still, despite the assurance, Carol felt shy and nervous about discussing the issue with Madam Juliet. Looking at the girl fidgeting nervously with the collar of her blouse, Juliet couldn't help remembering her own first love. It seemed like an entire lifetime had passed ever since. Ralph Newton... they had both been in high school then. She still felt that lurch, that sharp tug at her heart, yet it had been ages ago. She had had such a mad crush on the boy, but it was never meant to be. She had gone to Ghana after high school, as a volunteer with the Peace Corps following the dream she had had for a long time to visit the mysterious 'Dark Continent' she had heard of and read about. She had not seen many black people personally by then.

She had fallen in love with Ghana...and met someone who made the adolescent crush she had had on Ralph slowly fade away. She had been sure she had found her true love in Kwabena Agyeman. Tall dark Benny, as she had called him, with the deep captivating baritone that made her skin break out in goose bumps, and his hair parted at the left side. Ralph usually parted his on the right. And that was just one of the ways in which Benny was quite the opposite of Ralph.

Ralph had belonged to one of the oldest moneyed families in Duncan, going way back to around the time of the Treaty of Paris. He had been handsome in the correct way, tall, with wavy blonde locks and deep, sea blue eyes that you felt you could wade in and drift away to some faraway fantasy world. In contrast, it was almost impossible to see through

Benny's flint black eyes that never ceased to dance from one point to another, as if testing, tasting and weighing everyone and everything around him, without giving anyone else the slightest chance to do the same to him.

As much as she had seen him as the African prince of her fantasies, all Benny had been was the son of a village farmer, whose exceptional brilliance a missionary couple had noticed. They had seen him through school, including six months in Britain for a clerical course. The six months, however, did not erase some of his deep-rooted cultural tendencies which she had eventually found herself unable to cope with. Then it had been back home to Canada and college for her, by which time Ralph had moved on and had another girl in his life.

Then she had met Hezbon, the quiet, bespectacled, scholarly bookworm with a slight stammer. He seemed so bewildered and lost in a strange world; a kind of fish out of water. She had still had this fondness for Africa and Africans, and having lived in Africa, she felt like she understood him. That was why she had taken it upon herself to show him around and make him feel at home, and before she had known it, she was in love again! This time it had ended in a small civil wedding which her parents and most of her family had boycotted, and a lovely daughter.

Her heart had remained firmly with him even after discovering the truth about him when they relocated to Kenya, and even now that he had been dead almost nineteen years. That is how love goes; joy, pain, wrong turnings along the way, surprises—some pleasant and some not at all — around each bend in the long trail that love travels upon. She understood what Carol must feel, with the empathy of one who had worn the shoe in question.

"Anything else you need me to do Madam?" Carol asked suddenly, making Madam Juliet start a bit as she came out of her journey of memories.

"Errmm... nothing really, dear," she smiled gently at the girl.

Carol's perfect, clear English impressed her so much. Perhaps it was because she had gone to very good schools in the city before coming to live in the village. Even after living among them for so long, Juliet still had to strain a little to understand people from the village when they spoke their heavily-accented English. Sometimes they meant something quite different from what you would understand them to be saying.

"I was telling you dear, I was, you know, on the telephone with Lindsey last evening about your friend. She will contact someone she knows at the embassy to see what can be done. In the meantime, keep it under wraps, if you know what I mean."

Carol could have sworn she saw Madam Juliet wink slyly as she told her that in a conspiring tone. The old lady was so mysterious and full of surprises sometimes.

"By the way, I also talked to Lindsey about you, and — you know — the problems your family had, and she promised to talk to a lawyer about it too."

Carol felt another surge of warmth go through her... and a lightening. She always felt like she was carrying around something on her shoulders, and Madam Juliet's words seemed to lighten some of the weight.

"Where is that place you said your parents bought the land? Shakomoa...?"

"Syokimau," Carol quickly corrected her. "Yes, Dad... errmm...my late father said he had all the documents, although after he...died, Mum couldn't trace them. They just disappeared, then she got sick and... and..." Carol started feeling overwhelmed by feelings again and had to wipe her eyes with the back of her hand.

"It's okay dear; we shall see what can be done. I'm sure something can be done. And, if you don't mind me asking, didn't your parents have any kind of insurance...health insurance, life insurance, that sort of thing? From what you have told me about your father, it seems to me like he was the kind of person who would take care of such details."

Carol had never thought about that. She had been told at the hospital that her mother had used up all her medical insurance, but they had not even asked if her father had had any. As far as Carol knew, all contact with her father's former employers ended after they helped her family transport his body home and took care of his hospital bill and burial expenses. Carol had not even thought of asking if her mother had followed up his benefits or anything. She had been too young and overwhelmed by so many things that had happened too fast. Then her mother had become sick and couldn't be expected to help with anything.

"I have no idea at all Madam," she said in a small voice.

"Do you think you could get me the details about this bank where your father worked and their contacts?" Madam Juliet asked gently.

"I have a file where I keep the few documents we came here with, I'm sure I will find something."

Carol fervently hoped she would be able to find something. Perhaps there was a way out after all! Now she strongly suspected that her mother had been too confused to take care of a lot of the details she should have when her dad passed on. But her mum couldn't be blamed. Her father had always taken care of everything—even the grocery shopping! He had treated her mother the same way he treated their children— he had showered them all with attention and love. He had been their foundation and their pillar. Without him, everything had simply toppled over. Carol, now that she was older than she had been at the time, understood how confused and dazed her mother must have been.

"Please get me the documents as soon as possible dear," Madam Juliet reminded her as she left.

She had a hunch too, that there were a lot of things that had never been taken care of concerning the poor girl and the tragic turn of events with her parents. She really hoped that Lindsey would be able to take care of things for her. Madam Juliet had noticed the silent struggle the girl went through, although she tried really hard to hide it from everyone. She turned wearily in her armchair and brought her legs closer to the electric heater that Carol had turned on for her. She wished she had the energy she had once had so many years ago. Now she felt tired all the time.

She knew it would not be long before she joined Hezbon... her Bonny in heaven. She looked at the large framed photograph on the mantelpiece, which she always kept dusted and sparkling clean. She smiled to herself. Sometimes she still felt Hezbon's presence all around her. Perhaps that was why she would hear none of her daughter's advice to relocate to Vancouver. She was not sure that she would feel Hezbon's invisible presence as much as she did in the home they had shared. She knew it was rather childish and foolish to think that way, but she had become more sentimental than reasonable with time. She clung to the little, simple things that mattered most to her and made her happy.

9

It takes courage

To get what should be done

A little push

To help you take off

That is what courage is;

A kick in the behind

A shove to set you on the way

A splash in the face

To wake you up

Tough though it may seem

But what you need just then.

~Birdsong

Carol doubted that she and Saidi would be able to come up with a project for the science congress after all. There seemed to be so many things to think about and do besides that. Lately, she just couldn't think straight.

Besides, she was sure Saidi would not be around at the time the congress was scheduled to take place. That is, she was sure, until Saidi himself made her think otherwise.

"Even if I am going to die, let me die doing the things that have to be done," he had said with a hint of his usual humor, which she rarely heard nowadays.

"Who said you were going to die?" she asked as they slowly walked towards her home from the market, where she had gone to buy a few bunches of *murenda* for the day's supper.

"You have been going around with a long face like this," he made a comically sad face at her, "ever since I told you about Mustafa... you make me feel as if I were already dead!"

Carol screamed with laughter.

"Come on... I don't look long-faced!!"

She hit him lightly with the polythene bag holding the vegetables.

"How do you know, can you see your own face?" he asked her.

"You are such a jerk," she said, still laughing. It was such a relief to be able to laugh. She couldn't remember when she last had such a good, hearty laugh.

"But seriously, life goes on, we have to come up with a project. Madam Juliet is depending on us, whether the weight of the entire world is resting on our shoulders or not," Saidi said from the corner of his mouth, the way he talked when he was being serious about something.

"Okay, you come up with an idea, you are the man. You have always said that chemistry and sciences are generally men's subjects."

"And you, my dear Madame Curie, have always claimed chemistry for the fair sex. Now you come up with the ideas, and the big bad man will do the listening," Saidi made an exaggerated sweeping bow that made Carol laugh out loudly again.

"You should be a comic, not the scientist you want to be," she said between laughs.

Both of them were so absorbed in their cheerful banter that they did not notice a couple of people slowly walking up to them until they were almost right beside them. The taller of the two men pointedly cleared his throat and Carol's cheerful laughter died a sudden death in her throat.

"Mustafa!" Saidi gasped.

Carol looked at the two men, both of them young—in their late twenties at most. They were both dressed in long kanzus that came below their knees. The taller one's was a cold, metallic grey while the other had on a brown one. Carol guessed right away that the one in the grey kanzu was Mustafa, whom she had heard quite a lot about. She had never looked into the eyes of a snake, but she guessed that a snake's cold stare must be exactly like what she saw in Mustafa's cold eyes then. His whole appearance seemed so snake-like. He was very slim and quite tall, Carol felt like she was literally looking up to him—she had to raise her face to be able to meet his stare. His light-complexioned face was so thin that you could see his cheekbones clearly through the taut skin. Something about him reminded her of Kadesa, and she immediately had the unpleasant feeling that came whenever she saw, heard or thought about Kadesa, only stronger. The man seemed to exude some sort of evil from somewhere inside him

"*Assalam aleikum*," Saidi mumbled with the fear he felt clear in his voice. Both men ignored his greeting.

"Is this the *kafir* girl I have heard about?" Mustafa asked, sending a poisonous glance in Carol's direction.

"This is Carol, we are in the same class at school," Saidi said in a fearful voice.

Carol had never seen Saidi looking that scared. He was not a person that got easily scared. In spite of her fear , she could feel a spark of anger at what the man had called her, right when she was standing there listening to him. She had read somewhere that 'kafir' was a demeaning word that black people were referred to by the white people in South Africa during the despicable Apartheid era.

"Sir, please don't call me that."

The spark of anger had thawed the cold fear she had felt at first. The shorter man in the brown kanzu actually gasped with shock, as if she had said something astonishing. Carol looked at him for the first time. He had a wide face with a wide, shiny scar across the bridge of his nose.

"What?!"

Mustafa looked at her, his eyes becoming colder and more snake-like. But beyond the angry look, Carol could see what was clearly doubt in the man's eyes. It was as if he was so used to instilling fear and terror that he couldn't believe anyone, especially not a petite slip of a girl could stand up to him. Carol felt bolder then than she ever remembered feeling before.

"I don't like you calling me what you just called me," she said, staring straight into his face.

"Carol!" Saidi exclaimed in shock.

Carol turned and looked at him. His face looked so different, kind of contorted, with fear. This only made Carol bolder. If this was the same Mustafa that was bent on destroying Saidi's life, then she wanted to give him a good piece of her mind now that she had the chance.

"You cannot just go around bullying people and calling them names, you know, and forcing them to do things they don't want to," Carol found herself saying before she could stop herself.

She was simply tired. Tired of being bullied and pushed around by people. Tired of being tossed from place to place and enduring things she had no control over. She just wanted to let it all out. She had learned in one of the history classes about a woman named Rosa Parks, who had inspired black people in the United States of America to stand up for their rights by refusing to get up from her bus seat for a white person. Now she was sure she knew exactly how that lady must have felt. There is a limit to what someone can take from other human beings.

"Shut up!" the man in the brown kanzu suddenly shouted, while looking sideways at Mustafa, as if he wanted a pat on the back or some other congratulatory gesture from the man who was obviously his leader. But Mustafa only glared angrily at Carol, his nostrils flaring with his heavy breathing. Carol returned the man's stare squarely, without blinking once. In the end it was Mustafa who turned his face away. This was a battle between right and wrong and wrong knew that it had to give up under the onslaught of right.

"Come!" he hissed at Saidi in a choked voice before grabbing him by the arm and dragging him away, with the other man struggling to keep up with their pace.

He tried to give Carol what he may have meant to make a vicious look, but which turned into one of embarrassment and nervousness when Carol also stared him down. She was so angry, she wanted to go right after them, wrench Saidi's arm out of Mustafa's grasp and take him away to safety, away from those horrible people. All she could do, however, was stand there, her chest heaving with the heavy breathing that her great anger caused.

As the anger drained from her, she started realizing what she had done. Had she put Saidi in even more grave danger by what she had just done? Perhaps it had not been a very smart thing to do. She could instinctively tell that Mustafa was the kind of man who could do anything to other people without caring. What if she had endangered her own life and those of her mother, brother and sister apart from Saidi's?

She slowly bent down and picked up the polythene bag containing the vegetables she had been carrying. She hadn't even noticed that she had dropped it! She slowly started trudging along the path back home. Every few minutes, she would turn and glance behind her. She wasn't sure whether it was from the fear of seeing Mustafa following her, or the hope of seeing Saidi to reassure her. As if sensing the deathlike feeling in the air, some mousebirds in the bushes started chirping in alarmed tones;

Wa! Wa! Wa!

Lukuzu lukuchindura!

Lukuzu lukuchindura!

* * *

"Tomorrow I will be taking Form Four Yellow for a double lesson..." Carol's mother said suddenly, interrupting Big Susy's constant chatter.

"What is she saying? You know, me, I saw school from the path that passes behind it," Big Susy rasped in her hoarse voice.

Carol almost giggled but caught herself in time. She looked at her mother, her heart beating slightly faster with rising hope.

"And what will you be teaching Mum?" she asked gently and clearly.

She really wanted her mother to recover her memory, maybe this was the beginning. Perhaps she was remembering who she was. Her face was set with grim determination, as if she was determined to hold onto whatever wisps of her memory that were drifting back.

"The River and the Source..." she mumbled uncertainly; the set-book that that her students had been studying when she was still teaching.

A gush of hope surged through Carol's soul. Everything that had happened earlier in the evening at the confrontation with Mustafa was pushed instantly to the back of her mind, and so was the important news that Big Susy had come to tell her. Her mother's memory was coming back! Or was it? Since the traumatic incident that had happened about a week before, she had been a bit quiet and inactive, and Carol had assumed it had been because of the medication she was taking. The doctor had told Carol that the medication would have side-effects, like nausea and vomiting, and perhaps even fainting spells.

"Has she recovered?" Big Susy asked in a lower voice, her plain face becoming all solemn and serious.

"I think she is getting better," Carol replied wishfully, hoping with all the strength in her body for it to be true—for her words to trigger the miracle for which she was wishing with all the strength in her.

But trying so hard to remember seemed to have completely drained her mother of all energy. She slowly lowered herself onto the bed on which she had been sitting and turned her face to the wall.

"May God hear our prayers. You know, no illness is worse than this…" Big Susy slowly shook her head.

"So, you were saying that Uncle wants to take the shamba for himself?" Carol resumed the conversation they had been having before her mother's words had distracted her attention.

"Yes! He knows that *serikali* wants to buy land and build houses for people who work," Big Susy furtively looked around to see if anyone was eavesdropping.

"The chief said so during a *baraza*," she confided. "The government is going to take all this land, from near the main road down to the river. All the people who own it will be given larger portions of land in a settlement scheme, or money to buy some other land elsewhere," Big Susy gabbled excitedly. "Now, Jakobo wants to write down all the land that was your father's as his own."

Carol suddenly felt utterly drained and hopeless. How on earth was she going to deal with all that? A lot of things were happening that she needed to deal with, and each seemed even greater than the one before. How on earth was she ever going to take on her uncle? The whole world was going to take sides with him, no doubt.

"So what do I do now?" she asked Big Susy, hating the whiny sound of her own voice.

"Jakobo is claiming that your father did not leave a grown-up son, so he will take everything and hold it for you in the meantime, but even I can see he wants everything for himself, nothing else!" Big Susy gesticulated with the stems of murenda that she was holding in her hand. She was helping Carol to pluck the vegetables as they talked.

"What about Grego?" Carol asked in the same whiny voice, "Won't he grow up some day?"

She also wondered why only boys were considered someone's children. Even if there had only been her and Paulette, wouldn't they be entitled to whatever their late father owned? And then there was her mother, still alive and needing care. Why was her Uncle Jacob so unfair and selfish? Couldn't he even consider the sale of the land? Everything and everyone seemed so unfair.

"That is what you should tell the chief," Big Susy tapped her on the shoulder again with the vegetable stems.

"The chief?!" Carol exclaimed with dismay, the murenda she had been holding dropping into the small plastic basin on the ground between them.

"Yes! You should report this to the chief. Jakobo told him that he was doing this with your knowledge and that all he is going to do is hold the money for you until Asena grows up, but don't you need the money now? You should tell the chief this!" Big Susy's voice was getting hoarser and raspier, the harder she tried to make Carol see her point. She always called Gregory by his middle name.

Slowly, Carol started warming up to the idea of seeing the chief. Her father would want her to do exactly that, she thought. She was all that her remaining family had then. She was the 'man' of the home, who had to take care of such matters. It didn't matter what she thought or the fears she felt. This was part of her responsibility—what should be done.

"Will you go with me… please?" she inclined her head a bit to the right as she said that in a small, little-girl voice. She really needed Big Susy to go with her. Partially because she knew all too well that Big Susy would do most of the talking anyway, and so she would be saved the agony of trying to figure out what to say to the chief and how to say it. That and having Big Susy with her gave her courage and confidence to face anything.

"Is that a question or an answer?" Big Susy confirmed her eagerness to accompany Carol to the chief's office, smiling her warm, broad smile that exposed the gap in her upper front teeth, where one of her teeth had been extracted so many years before.

Big Susy had certainly never been pretty or beautiful all her life in the way that most people thought 'beautiful' was and she could not exactly be called 'smart'— she had not been to school much, but she had a heart the size of a house. That was the beauty that God had given her. She was always there to cheer up, to comfort, share and to help in the small, simple ways she could, and that — a lot of the time—is how people really need to be helped. Very often, all someone needs is someone to be there with them and listen, even if they do not understand.

10

A new day

Another bend in the road

A new sun

A new ray of hope

A treasure chest,

just waiting to be opened

A surprise, an unopened gift.

 ~Birdsong

The sound of birdsong is what makes the mornings in the countryside even more beautiful and captivating. Each new day—with a new golden shining sun of its own — like a newly minted coin to be spent or squandered as each person would, is heralded by a burst of cheerful, jubilant birdsong. This self-assured outpouring of joy comes from hundreds of creatures so small and weak as to be totally unimportant, yet the little creatures seemed to understand that there is someone big and great up there somewhere looking out for them. To them, just making it to another day is a miracle worth celebrating and singing for joy, and they greet the arrival of every day with these moving choruses, each bird with its own song to sing. Kui Ndenga had heard several times people quoting the part of the Bible that says not a single sparrow falls that God is not aware of. That God feeds the little creatures, the fact that they did not cultivate land or harvest grain notwithstanding.

In the days of confusion during her illness, the only thing that brought Kui total joy were the lusty sounds the birds made. She had been born and raised in the city, in the crowded estates of Nairobi's Eastlands area where no sound of birdsong or nature generally could ever be heard. Instead, there was the constant roar of smoke-belching vehicles of different sizes and types and the voices of hordes of human beings. That had been her life for most of the years that she had been alive. Busy roads with traffic issues and crowded rental houses with lots of people stuck with each other were all she knew, until she had had the chance to move to a better place.

Ever since the day she had been assaulted near the market, Kui had started swimming in and out of her brief moments of clarity more often. For brief moments her mind would clear up and she would wonder if she would be having her lessons that day and if she had prepared her schemes of work. Or all of a sudden, she would think that there was a continuous assessment test to prepare for her students. She had often joked to her students, whenever a C.A.T was due, to prepare because "I'm going to unleash a cat on your mousy selves tomorrow" or something like that. That was the kind of humour and cheer that came naturally to her and endeared her so much to her students.

Sometimes, the names of her colleagues and students and the images would drift in and out of her mind. Through all of it, there was one pleasant feeling that was there all the time. The warm feeling which she associated with the pleasant girl who fed her and made her take her bath. In her more clear moments, Kui understood that it was her daughter, her eldest child Caroline. A lot of the time though, she thought the girl was her own mother, who had passed on years ago when she was a girl herself. This was mostly because Carol brought back that feeling of comfort and security, the 'Mum is back' feeling that is so important to every child. Her illness had made her become a child once more, forcing her to switch places with her child, who now did all the mothering that had to be done.

Seated on a low stool outside the small hut in which she and her children now lived, Kui could smell the pleasant scent that drifted from a small shrub with clusters of small, cream-colored flowers along each of its branches. It always exuded that pleasant smell in the nights and early mornings. The sun was still new and rising over the horizon and not warm enough to drive away the morning chill and so Carol had wrapped a woolen shawl around her shoulders to keep her warm. She had to sit outside for a while as Carol tidied up the house.

Somewhere near her brother-in-law's house, a rooster kept calling out Guri-guu-gu-guu!! at intervals, never growing tired of celebrating the dawn of a new day.

In the bushes around her hut, a couple of mouse-birds boasted of their smartness and slyness to each other and to the other birds saying,

'Vogeri, vogeri likorove!

Vogeri, vogeri likorove!'

Near them, a smaller, brown-colored bird kept up a cheerful

Flip-flop three!

Slip-slap three!

Chip-chop three!

In the tall tree just next to her hut the determined persistent knocking of yet another early bird, a woodpecker, searching for insects in the bark of the tree carried over very clearly. In the hedge that separated the hut from Jacob's house a few hundred metres away, Kui could hear the clear tones of the bird she liked most, calling out the usual song in a gregarious, upbeat manner;

Good boy toto!

Bring back toto!

Good job toto!

Great, great toto!

Perhaps the 'words' of this bird's song appealed a lot to Kui because even in her illness, she had her maternal feelings. She thought of the bird as a mother like herself, although it was her nestlings that now had to look for food and bring it back to her, not the other way round as it should be.

"Come and take your porridge now, Mum," Carol stuck her head around the door and told her.

Kui did not feel like eating anything. She felt so poorly and exhausted lately, and she had started vomiting often in the mornings. All the same, she slowly got up and walked into the house. She always obeyed Carol.

Carol tasted a bit of the porridge to make sure that it was not too hot before handing it to her mother. She was a little anxious that day because it was the day when the chief was going to hold a baraza meeting to discuss the land that her uncle Jacob was claiming. She had not wanted it to become such a big issue. She wished she hadn't let Big Susy talk her into it. Perhaps she should just have let Jacob do whatever he wanted.

The previous evening, Gregory had been chased away from Uncle Jacob's house and told by their Aunt Rispa to never go back there again. Carol felt so guilty about it. She knew just how much Gregory enjoyed playing with his cousins and watching the programs he really liked on the old, fourteen-inch 'Sanyo' T.V that their Uncle Jacob had, which was powered by a car battery.

She looked outside and watched Gregory silently walking along the hedge that divided their house from their uncle's, furtively glancing over at their uncle's house. It was Saturday, so there was no school that day. Carol knew that Gregory would be in for one boring weekend now that he couldn't play with his cousins, whom he had grown so close to over the time they had lived there.

"Grego!" she called out to him.

He immediately started walking towards the house in silent obedience.

"Why do you look so bored?" she asked gently, removing a piece of dried leaf from his hair before starting to pat him on the head.

Gregory shook her hand off. She had forgotten that he really disliked being treated like a small kid, often declaring that he was a 'big person'.

"I wanted to go and watch my program on VTV," he said sulkily, "but you reported Uncle to the chief, and now he hates me too!"

"Oh, *woiyee* Grego..." Carol felt even more rotten.

For a moment, she wished she had thought some more about Big Susy's advice and talked to Madam Juliet about it first. She had never imagined that doing what she had to could cause so much hurt to other people. Anyway, it had been the right thing to do! It was Uncle Jacob who was wrong. He had no right to take what was not his. Being right has its consequences too, the toughest being that it may make some people hate you. When you stand up for the truth, there will always be the backlash from those who do not feel the same as you to deal with.

"Don't worry, we will soon have our own television," she said without believing it herself.

"When? You don't have enough money to buy one," Greg said sulkily.

It struck Carol then that Greg automatically saw her as the one who could buy him a television set, who would solve problems.

"Don't worry, okay? I will find some money, we will move away from here, and we will buy our own T.V."

Carol had been fourteen; just a year older than Greg now was, when she had started taking care of everyone else. But Greg seemed such a small kid still! Perhaps it was true that girls grew up faster than boys, or that first-borns matured faster than the other children. She felt a sudden flood of affection welling up as inside her as she looked at Greg. He looked so much like their late father... a bit too tall for his age, he was certainly going to be tall and sturdy the way their dad had been.

"Why are you looking at me that way?" Greg asked, looking uncomfortable.

Carol laughed and looked away. The bonds of blood. Looking at her younger brother gave her a rush of feelings of affection that she could never feel for anyone else apart from her two siblings and her mother. She would go to every length to take care of them, protect them and make them happy. She would walk over coals of fire and confront any beast that threatened them. And that was why she was going to that baraza to speak for them. No one else would if she did not. Paulette, who had still been sleeping, came out of the hut yawning and rubbing her eyes as she went around to the back of the hut, obviously to answer a call of nature.

"Sasa sweetie! Did you dream of anything nice?" Carol called out to her as cheerfully as she could, despite the fact that what she was feeling that morning was anything but cheerful.

Perhaps it is an inborn instinct that is in every girl and woman, always there and waiting to be activated, to put other people's interests before her own. No one had taught Carol, ever. She had just learnt to hide her true feelings from her brother and sister if the feelings were not pleasant. It had come to her notice that whenever she was sad, anxious, afraid or angry, it usually affected her siblings too, and so she tried as much as she could to always show them a happy face. That was what they needed most of all.

"Good morning," Paulette answered, yawning sleepily.

"She was coughing at night," Gregory pointed out, still keeping his voice sulky and the dour look firmly on his face.

Carol smiled gently at him. How cute, she thought to herself. He also cared about his little sister, never mind the fact that he was also carrying the very weight of the world on his shoulders now that he was going to miss one precious episode of 'his' program.

"I will buy her some cough syrup at the medicine duka," Carol told him, still smiling gently.

Greg had already taken his breakfast, and she had kept Paulette's porridge ready for her in the pink mug with a bunny on it, which she liked so much. Breakfast was brown millet and sorghum porridge, with just a hint of sugar because it had to be made to last as long as possible. Ironically, circumstances had forced them to be eating healthier than they had when they were financially well-off. Breakfast back then would be tea or coffee with eggs, white bread and margarine or butter, sometimes with sausages, eggs or even fried meat. Carol caught herself salivating as she remembered.

Paulette never gave any indication of remembering when they ate different food, and Greg had given up complaining and refusing to eat after a couple of months. Now he devoured boiled plantain and roasted cassava just as greedily as he had tucked into a pizza or hot-dogs when he was younger. Perhaps it was a boy thing, the way he so quickly adjusted and coped faster than she did. She knew that by the time the day ended, he would be running around and playing football with some other boys with a ball made from dry banana fronds and discarded polythene bags. He was bound to find some other play-mates even if their cousins could no longer play with him. He was a tough little survivor—he would live.

"Grego...*shika*(here)!" she said suddenly, fishing out a five- shilling coin from the pocket of her dress and handing it to her brother. He sure needed some motivation.

"What?" he asked, still in the dour tone as he took the coin from her. He had assumed that she was sending him to the shop to get something.

"It's yours. Get some sweets or something." She patted his head again, but very briefly, so as not to embarrass him again.

The slight hint of a smile that flitted across his face, like a light breeze sweeping away dark clouds from the face of the sun, was all the reward she needed. She went back inside the hut to prepare for the baraza. Seeing her brother, mother and sister had somehow emboldened her. She had to do it for them. It had to be done somehow.

* * *

"I told you so," Big Susy whispered, her voice of course being heard for several metres around her.

"Shhhh!" someone hissed sharply in a startlingly snake-like manner from behind them.

Carol knew right away that it was Kadesa. Even that brief sound meant to shut them up was full of hostility. Why did the woman come to the baraza anyway? Perhaps she thought

Carol would be humiliated and have her family's land taken away and she had come to gloat.

"It is only when a person passes on without leaving any child at all that his brothers are allowed to take the land that would have been his," the chief was saying in a deep baritone.

Carol exhaled as a feeling of relief swept through her heart. For a moment during the hearings, she had really feared that things would go her uncle's way. She had not expected so many people to be at the baraza. She had not even been fully aware what it was going to be like. She had imagined that there was only going to be her uncle and her, and perhaps her aunt and Big Susy at the baraza. But half the village had turned up. Most of the crowd sat down on the grass in front of the chief's office, with some — mostly the men and boys — standing behind those who were sitting.

It had been a lot like Miss Sagala's courtroom drama back at school, only that this was so serious and grown-up. First of all, her uncle had been called to speak, and he had done so, in the local language, so much of what he said was lost to Carol. What she couldn't help noticing, however, was the pretence that he was such a nice, well meaning person who had the interests of his nieces, nephew and his sick sister-in-law at hand. He made it look as if he had been taking very good care of them ever since his late brother passed on, and being in control of the money from the land was just part of the whole responsibility he had over them — with the children being so small and his sister ill and all that.

After his very long speech, which was interrupted a number of times by jeers and at some point laughter from the audience; Carol was at last, called upon to speak. Her heart had pounded like the frenzied drums of some of the religious sects. This was made even worse by the fact that as soon as she scrambled onto her feet, several voices shouted at her to sit down. This made her so confused that for a moment, she just stood there bewildered until Big Susy tugged at her dress and told her to sit down.

"Women are supposed to speak while sitting down," she explained in a low hiss.

In the midst of her panic, Carol wondered why Big Susy had not told her about this important protocol. But it suited Carol just fine. Her fear was to have to stand in front of the large crowd. Not trusting her grasp of the local language, Carol had decided to speak in Kiswahili, her voice becoming stronger and more confident as she explained. She knew that she was right. She was speaking the simple truth and all she had to do was be clear and just explain herself. She did not have the eloquence, experience or slyness of her uncle who —unlike her—was allowed by tradition to stand before the people and walk around as he pleased, but she had the truth, and truth stands up above every lie.

"We ... my mother, brother and sister have never received any kind of help from Uncle as he is saying," Carol explained. "He cannot claim to have developed a sudden interest in helping us now that there is money to be given for the land.

I respect him a lot, but I am old enough to handle matters concerning the land. I have had to deal with bigger matters than that, and whenever I run into difficulties, I will be willing to ask for his assistance."

The crowd listened to her soft but very clear voice attentively. She had been afraid of getting booed or heckled, but that never happened. Much to her relief, most of the people who gave their opinion seemed to side with her. Although the chief was a government-appointed administrator, he was regarded by the village folk as the traditional leaders must have been in the olden days. In fact most of the people – including Big Susy – referred to the barazas as *uluhya*; a council of elders. That was the same council system of administration that gave a group of sixteen related tribes of western Kenya their common name, the Baluhya.

The chief's word was final. And now the chief was giving his judgment; that Carol was going to be allowed into all consultations concerning the portion of land that had been her late father's. She was going to be assumed to be representing her younger brother, who was considered her father's heir as the tradition demanded.

Carol felt such a strong sense of accomplishment— she had done it! She had stood up for... okay – that was figurative. She had actually been required to sit down through it all, but then it had been a baraza sitting too, hadn't it? And she had defended her family's interests. She could almost feel her late father smiling down from somewhere up there.

"I told you so!" Big Susy grasped her arm.

"Why didn't you tell me I was supposed to speak while sitting down?" was all Carol could think of saying.

"I thought you knew!" Big Susy was genuinely surprised.

She had been raised in the village and spent all her life there. She had known such customs and elements of her culture all her life. She could not have imagined that someone else didn't know anything about these rules. Saidi sidled over to them from somewhere among the crowd.

"Phew! You are still alive!" Carol gave an exaggerated sigh of relief.

"No, I'm dead, this is my ghost at your service," he mumbled.

Carol couldn't help giggling. It was easier to laugh now that what she had been afraid of was now behind her.

"Now this is what they call victory. You showed them Madame Curie!" Saidi had his usual cheeky grin firmly in place. Carol clicked her tongue in mock annoyance.

"You are behaving as if it was you that handed me the so-called victory on a silver plate. By the way, how did it go with your brother the monster?"

"Cousin, not brother, there is a difference." Saidi waved a finger at her, his face suddenly becoming serious.

"Look Kaaro, let me go and prepare food for my children mwaana, I will come and see you later," Big Susy nudged Carol gently as she said that.

Carol was horrified to realise that she had forgotten all about the presence of her other friend.

"Okay Susy. *Haki* thank you so much for helping me," she squeezed her friend's hand, noticing the suspicious glances that Big Susy cast in Saidi's direction.

"Yep, bad influence. I can almost hear her think," Saidi said in a low voice.

"Stop suspecting yourself," Carol laughed in a low voice.

The crowd had started dispersing slowly and drifting away from the chief's office while loudly discussing the land matter and other things. The two of them also started to walk along the winding path that led to Carol's home. As soon as they had walked far enough, Carol looked around to make sure that no one was listening before giving Saidi the news that Madam Juliet had given her the previous evening.

"Madam Juliet's daughter, Lindsey — the one she speaks about all the time — will be organizing for you to be taken to a boarding school in Nairobi. You are not supposed to tell anyone about this, not even your mother," Carol whispered conspiringly.

"You are serious, aren't you?" Saidi stared at Carol.

She had not told him that she had talked to Madam Juliet about his problem with Mustafa because he would most likely have persuaded her not to.

"I'm dead serious," Carol looked at him straight in the face. "Okay, I knew you would stop me if I told you about it, so I just went ahead."

"What! Now you are putting not only your stubborn self in danger, but also that poor old lady! Don't you realize what kind of people Mustafa and his crowd are? They won't hesitate to kill anyone, they believe that the holy scriptures —God Himself— allows them to kill anyone who is in their way." Saidi was almost shouting in his exasperation.

"Hey, not so loud!" Carol looked around furtively. "Someone will hear you! Listen, as long as you cooperate, there is no way they will find out. You will simply disappear! And we will make sure we are not seen together just before you disappear, there is no way anyone will connect your going away with Madam Juliet — or me for that matter."

Carol could clearly see that Saidi was warming up to the idea fast. His face was literally lighting up. This was the ray of hope that he needed. His relief was compounded by the fact that now he was sure Carol and Madam Juliet wouldn't come to any harm for helping him.

"In the meantime, just behave as much as possible as if you are cooperating with Mustafa and his ...errmm... buddies, and as if you are very much for the idea of joining those mujibeen."

"Mujahideen."

"Whatever!" Carol retorted playfully. "By the way, you can make quite a good one with those pirate eyes and scary face," she teased.

Saidi hooted with laughter before he could stop himself. Then he stopped himself and looked anxiously around them, but the crowd that had attended the baraza had completely dispersed and the path was deserted.

"By the way, about the chemistry project, have you had any ideas yet–Marie Curie?" Saidi asked in a more serious tone.

"Not yet, what about you? The man... remember?" Carol grinned.

"Ha-ha! Funny!" Saidi rolled his eyes. "Look, why don't we ask Magwaro for help?"

"You are kidding, right?" Carol asked after she had stared at him for a few minutes.

"Do I look like I'm kidding?"

"The same person I am thinking of?" Carol asked doubtfully.

"Yes, the husband of your bosom friend Kadesa—he is a Chemistry whiz you know."

Carol could see that Saidi seemed quite serious as he said that and she couldn't help laughing out loud at that.

"Stop trying to be funny, look, if we can't think of anything Madam Juliet will understand."

"No, I'm serious, Magwaro used to be one of the best chemistry teachers way back, he is a graduate teacher you know—BSc. He was suspended and later indicted because of his drinking problem."

"Like seriously?" Carol still couldn't believe it, even after she was sure Saidi wasn't kidding.

"Like seriously!" Saidi mimicked her voice, making her lose her wide-eyed, gape-mouthed surprised look and burst into laughter again.

"Okay, whatever. You ask him, I don't want more trouble from you-know-who."

She somehow couldn't bring herself to say Kadesa's name.

"You think she will scratch your eyes out and think you are going to snatch her man? Oh, please!"

"I just don't want any trouble from anyone, please, and I have seen him in action once, I don't want to go anywhere near him."

"He is only that way when drunk," Saidi assured her. "We can go and see him early in the morning, when he has not yet started drinking. By the way, I don't think Kadesa is as bad as you always make her sound."

"What!"

"Okay, just kidding, I know what she is like, but the way someone behaves towards us should not dictate how we behave towards them. You shouldn't let anyone change you into what you are not," Saidi said in a rather solemn tone.

"Hmmm... spitting wisdom today are we?" Carol smiled warmly at him.

Looking at his light-skinned face, she felt once more, the warm glow, the flow of good feelings that she always felt towards him. Perhaps this was love, the thing she had read and heard about for so long, and seen in movies and plays. Could Saidi be the 'first love' that Madam Juliet had spoken to her about? They came from such different worlds, although even that, they had in common.

11

Look under the cover

That is where it is

A new discovery,

that has been there all along

The top may not talk much

But underneath speaks volumes

What you see upfront

That is just what you see.

~Birdsong

No one and nothing could have dragged Carol to Kadesa's home—not even wild horses. She made that very clear to Saidi. There was absolutely no way she was going to go there. If Saidi was insisting that they talk to Magwaro, Kadesa's drunken husband, then it had to be somewhere else away from his home. And it was at the small kiosk at the junction, just a few metres away from Hillside

Academy — an open public place where people could come to one's aid if at some point one screamed for help, as Carol pointed out, much to Saidi's amusement.

"First of all, you will need to make the soap itself. The ingredients would be sodium tallowate or sodium cocoate, but sodium palm kernelate could also do splendidly. Then water of course and sodium chloride, sodium silicate, magnesium sulfate and a fragrance of your choice. They are available in supermarkets and places like that in Kisumu—I'm sure the mzungu teacher will be able to get them."

Carol didn't notice that she was staring at Magwaro with her mouth wide open until Saidi nudged her sharply.

"Huh!? Oh, yes, of course, I'm sure she will," Carol stammered.

She just couldn't believe her eyes. Magwaro, unshaved and dressed in dirty rags, was talking so fluently and flawlessly, and seemed very much at home with the chemical terminology as he explained the process for them. It had been Carol's idea that they do a project that was simple but useful and applicable to the village folk. Magwaro had suggested making soap that expands when subjected to heat. In that way, people could double their soap and significantly reduce their domestic budget. It was these simple things that really mattered to them.

Although a strong smell of rancid sweat, sour body odour, vomit, urine and grime wafted from him right to where Carol was seated a couple of metres away, she couldn't help feeling a sudden sense of respect for him. Now she believed what Saidi had told her before, that Magwaro had been a chemistry teacher, a Bsc graduate. It was obvious, however, that none of what he had learned had been 'rubbed away from his brain' as Big Susy had said before. Beneath all the grime and stench was a brain that could still be useful to him and to others. Carol remembered her Aunt Gracie. She had also been exceptionally brilliant, according to her mother, but addiction to alcohol and drugs had prevented her from being all that she could have become.

She watched Saidi scribbling away with a lot of concentration inside the folded notebook he had on his knee. The teacher in Magwaro had been fully aroused, with students sitting in front of him listening and taking notes. He talked in a calm, clear voice, a bit scratchy from the effect of harsh spirits perhaps, and too much yelling around the village. His shaggy, untidy head was held up with a dignity and confidence that welled up from somewhere deep inside him; a confidence that came from knowing, and knowing that he knew.

"Okay, that would be all, unless you have any questions."

He smiled a little smile that exposed a couple of broken and discolored front teeth.

"Uhmm, no... no, I think I got it all but in case we need anything more, we shall just ask you. Carol?" Saidi looked at her with one eyebrow raised.

"No, I'm okay," Carol answered in a daze.

"We are good then. Now! Let the teacher get his dues."

Magwaro rubbed his hands together and licked his lips in anticipation. There was a noticeable transformation— from the dignified, knowledge dispensing teacher, to a thirsty drunkard who couldn't wait to go and wet his throat. Carol had suspected that all his help was not going to be for free, and Saidi had come fully prepared. He fumbled about inside one of his pockets and took out a crumpled, rather shabby one hundred shilling - note which Magwaro all but snatched away from him before scrambling off the small bench, eager to get to his next drink.

"Yep. You were saying?" Saidi grinned cheekily at Carol as soon as Magwaro was out of earshot.

"I'm lost for words — *sisemi kitu*," Carol admitted truthfully. Magwaro's horrible body smell still lingered in her nose, but what lingered in her mind much more strongly was his impeccable, astounding grasp of Chemistry.

* * *

"I hope the owner of the wood knows you took it? We don't need any more trouble," Carol told Greg as she looked at the pile of dry firewood that he had brought home.

As much as she really appreciated it, she was a bit worried. Her family was not exactly a favourite with other people around the village and she didn't want anyone finding an excuse to subject them to any more harassment.

"I was with other kids...we asked for her permission. There was a lot of it just lying around her land near the river," Greg pointed out in the dour voice he had adapted lately, ever since he could no longer go to their uncle's.

Carol wondered whether it was just her imagination or his voice was deepening. He was growing up. Soon he was going to need a grown man to guide him and show him how to grow up into a man. Carol wondered who that was going to be, now that their uncle was not on good terms with them. When he had been able to be with his cousins and their uncle, she had hoped that somehow, he was going to learn whatever there was to be learned just by being close to them. Perhaps though, most of what he had to learn she could teach him and practically demonstrate as it was; responsibility and putting others before him; fighting for what was right even if it brought unpleasant consequences; not letting down those who depend on him and not taking even a stick of wood that he did not have any right to — that she could easily put across to him.

In a way, she was as much a man as any could be; even more than some men were. Just by bringing home firewood without being asked to find some, Carol knew that Greg had learned a lesson or two already. He knew he had to do what he could to help. She took the pile of wood inside the hut, where she was already cooking on the three-stoned hearth in the corner of one of the rooms.

She broke one of the longer pieces of wood in half and put both halves into the fire. That night she had something special. She had bought a quarter kilo of meat. Not much, but a special treat just the same. They hardly ever had meat, quite a contrast to when they had to choose between fish, beef, mutton or pork, sometimes rabbit or quail or game meat when her father could get it. Carol always stopped herself on dwelling on the past. It was no use at all.

She bent down, puffed up her cheeks and blew into the fire to make it glow brighter. She had eked out the meat with carrots and potatoes, and a packet of beef stock that she had bought for five shillings. Already, a savory, appetizing aroma was wafting from the saucepan, filling the entire hut and even drifting outside.

Her mother was lying quietly on the bed in the other room. Lately, Carol was quite afraid that the attack at the market place was making her revert to her former state, just before they had moved to the village. Maybe it was just the effect of the drugs she had to take. There was just a week to go before she could stop giving them to her. She had started vomiting in the mornings, and she didn't sing with the birds anymore. The only good thing was that she didn't roam aimlessly around the village as she used to. In fact she didn't do much except sleep, eat and sit sometimes in the sun for a few minutes. Carol peeked around the door and looked at her mother.

She was lying prone on the bed, and except for occasionally blinking, she didn't seem alive at all. Paulette was sprawled on the floor, scribbling in her books as she did most of the time. Greg had come in and seemed to be searching for something in the bag in which his clothes and other stuff was usually kept.

"Are you looking for something Grego?" Carol asked, looking for an opportunity to break the silence.

Before Greg could answer her, someone screamed loudly and shrilly just outside the house, the shrill sound startling them all almost out of their skin. Before they could react to the scream, the person who had apparently screamed suddenly burst into the room. It was a woman — and she was completely naked, crying and panting very fast. She jumped from the room in which Carol was straight into the other room, startling Carol's mother from her trance. They all screamed at the top of their voices from shock and fright. Carol's mother actually sprang from her bed and gave the loudest screams of all. The naked woman crouched in a corner of the room, panting heavily and sobbing loudly, all the while covering her face with her arms as if she expected someone to hit her or something.

"He wants to kill me... he will kill me!" she kept repeating over and over.

Carol didn't know what else to do, so she ran outside to scream for help...and came face to face with Magwaro, who was wielding a large *panga* just a couple of metres away from the door. She almost fainted, but Magwaro seemed a bit startled too on seeing her. It was as if he had not expected to see her there. It could be that he was not even aware that that was her home.

"Please don't kill me!" Carol squealed with fright, dropping to her knees and putting her arms onto her head.

She was sure the end had come, and she wildly wondered what it would feel like to be cut to death with a panga. What was going to happen to her mother? To Greg and Paulette? But Magwaro had lost interest in his chase and, mumbling drunkenly, turned and shuffled away, as Carol's Uncle Jacob, some women including her aunt and some of her cousins came running over. Carol collapsed onto the ground and started sobbing, more from relief than anything else.

"Eesu! He didn't even touch you! What are you crying about?" Carol's aunt wondered loudly before clicking her tongue, spitting on the ground and walking back to whatever she had been doing.

Carol tried to pull herself together.

"He was chasing someone...naked...inside the house," she panted, between sobs.

Her heart was pounding harder than it had ever done before.

"Kadesa," her uncle grunted in a matter-of-fact manner before turning on his heel and going back to his house. Most of the other people, sensing that the drama was mostly over, also left, murmuring and talking among themselves, some laughing openly in amusement.

"Kadesa?" Carol wondered out loud.

She got up from the ground and cautiously sneaked into the house. Paulette was still weeping loudly inside the house, but her mother had stopped screaming. Greg had followed her outside when he had heard her scream.

"Kadesa?" Carol called out softly.

The naked woman was still sobbing hysterically. Carol gingerly stepped into the room. It was Kadesa alright, as Carol saw when she turned her tear-streaked face towards her, although of course previously she had always seen her dressed in long dresses and headscarves, with a leso or shawl over her shoulders. She had foam and lather all over her—she had obviously been taking her bath or something when Magwaro had chased her. And her home was several compounds away! Carol quickly picked up a leso and handed it to Kadesa to cover herself up with, before searching for a blouse and skirt among her things and giving them to her.

"Thank you...thank you..." Kadesa whispered almost inaudibly.

Carol remembered at precisely that moment, something that Big Susy liked to say; " The good book says when your enemy is hungry, feed him! When he is naked clothe him." Carol had never imagined that the part about clothing her naked enemy would come to pass so literally! She turned to see if her mother was alright and knew right away that something had happened. Her mother's eyes seemed clearer, if a little bewildered.

"Carol?" she asked in a small voice, "Is it you? What happened, who is she, where are we?"

Carol could sense deep inside her that something had happened to her mother. She forgot everything about Kadesa, who was wearing the blouse and skirt she had been given, and rushed over to her mother, giving her a giant bear hug.

"Is that Polly crying?" her mother asked, before wriggling out of Carol's grasp and shuffling into the other room.

She was the only one who had ever called Paulette by that name. Paulette stopped sniffling as if she too had sensed the change in their mother and looked at her with her mouth slightly open and her eyes filled with a lot of unspoken questions. The smell of burning stew roused Carol from her wonderment and she rushed over to the hearth and lifted the saucepan of stew off the fire.

* * *

"It happens... it is a sort of shock treatment, sometimes it is even used in hospitals," Madam Juliet explained to Carol, wiping tears from her eyes.

She had had a hearty laugh after listening to Carol recounting to her what had happened at her home the previous evening and how her mother had suddenly been totally cured after the naked Kadesa had startled them so much.

Miss Sagala, who was also present, was still laughing. She had thrown back her head and her scarf had slipped, exposing a crop of luxuriant, thick black hair that reminded Carol of Saidi's. Madam Juliet had requested to meet them both at her house after school to discuss a few things.

"You know, Bonnie...errmm... my late husband, Hezbon once told me a similar story," Madam Juliet said. "He used to work in Naivasha, and there was a...you know...mentally ill man who used to roam around the town totally naked. Well, actually, he usually had a big woollen overcoat on, but whenever it got too hot, he would take it and hide it in the bushes near Lake Naivasha and just walk around without a stitch on."

Carol covered her mouth while pretending to brush away something, so that her teachers wouldn't see her smile. There was something so amusing about the way Madam Juliet said it.

"So, one day, a huge black snake crept into the overcoat and coiled inside while the man was taking his... you know, stroll around town," Madam Juliet continued. "When he came back for it in the evening and tried to put it on, the snake uncoiled itself and hissed loudly at him—he was so shocked that after he calmed down and stopped screaming, he was completely cured!

It's a true story but I am told that is the method witchdoctors and even some so-called faith healers use to perform their miracles. It is a sort of hypnotism. The human mind is so complex and delicate that a shock from a traumatic experience could shut it down or jump-start its functions—and all of the body's functions are controlled by the brain; the mind. A lot of diseases that people suffer from are actually psychosomatic—rooted in their minds that is."

Carol thought of how she sometimes had to slap or sharply shake her tiny 'Cony' radio to make it function and how it at times just went off if someone walked too heavily near it.

"Well, good things just like bad things do not come in ones, apparently," Madam Juliet said, her usually rheumy eyes sparkling mischievously for a change.

"*Alhamdulillah*!" Miss Sagala raised her hands in thanksgiving.

Madam Juliet took the large envelope that had been lying on the coffee table in front of her and took out a sheaf of papers.

"Lindsey had someone with legal knowledge look up your case at your father's former employers. Apparently, no one followed up his dues."

She looked at some of the papers.

"There are his benefits from the National Social Security Fund, and his savings in the savings and credit society which no one followed up—did your mother know about it?" she asked.

"I don't think so. She kept on saying that Dad had taken a lot of loans and his payslip had practically nothing left over after the deductions. She said there was no way at all that his employers could owe him any dues. In fact she was always scared that they would come after us to arrest her or something, over Dad's debts."

"Poor her," Madam Juliet shook her head gravely, "she probably didn't have any idea, she must have been so overwhelmed by everything."

Miss Sagala clucked in sympathy.

"Then, were you aware that the owners of the homes that were demolished negotiated an out-of-court settlement with the government? According to this settlement, the homeowners are supposed to get some money by way of compensation."

Carol was totally speechless. She could only shake her head.

"Well, now you know!" Madam Juliet actually looked visibly younger as she said that.

She was someone who treasured the happiness she brought into other people's lives. Quite the opposite of what Kadesa had been, but then the poor woman had just wanted an outlet for the suffering she was going through at her abusive husband's hands.

"Now for some more good news!" Madam Juliet was on a roll, "Saidi's admission to Hakati Educational Centre has been confirmed. Munira, I'm sure you can, you know, arrange for his journey to Nairobi. Make sure it seems, you know, like he just disappeared and you have no idea how it happened… for everyone else's safety. We are not sure who and what we are dealing with at the moment."

"Sure! Consider it done! All this radicalism and mujahideen nonsense is something totally new! We have always been taught that our religion itself means peace…peace! Our holy book talks about peace and harmony with oneself and others," the fire of passion lit up her eyes as she spoke. "The real Jihad is something that begins with someone's lower soul—the negative feelings and emotions. If it is to be with those who do not believe in religion, the war should take a form that is acceptable and in harmony with law and justice like persuasion—the way you Christians do, preaching the word and evangelizing, that's what the holy Prophet—peace be upon him—taught. And, let me ask you, if God really didn't want anyone to live, would they remain alive? I believe He would know what to do about it—it's not as if He is a weak, powerless being we have to fight and kill for!"

It was as if Miss Sagala was in class, expounding and explaining. Madam Juliet shook her head solemnly.

"Such a shame Munira, that you will be quitting your teaching career soon—you are such a natural teacher."

"But a legal profession is my real passion, I have always wanted to be part of the justice system."

"When will you be completing your LLb, by the way?" Madam Juliet asked.

"Towards the end of next year *inshallah*," Miss Sagala confirmed.

As Carol could gather from the conversation, Miss Sagala had been studying for her Law degree through evening classes. Her hunch about her teacher's passion for legal matters had not been wrong after all! She couldn't help smiling to herself, remembering how Miss Sagala had handled the 'case' a few months back in class as she put the teacups they had been using on a silver tray and carried them into Madam Juliet's tiny kitchen.

Down the Line

A moment of silence in remembrance of the departed may not have been the ideal way to start a joyous occasion, but it really didn't take any of the cheer out of the auspicious evening. The hall hired for the occasion seemed to be filling up really fast, and Carol was beginning to wonder whether it was going to hold all the guests, invited and uninvited. They were not going to turn away anyone who wanted to attend the launch of *A burst of birdsong*, her mother's collection of poems.

She had thought that they would have to postpone or put off the occasion altogether after the horrific terrorist attack at Eastend shopping mall in an upmarket area of Nairobi earlier in the month, but after consulting with other people, they had decided to go ahead with it. Kwasi Agyeman, the world famous Ghanaian poet who had been expected to be the guest of honor at the launch was one of those who had perished in the vicious terrorist attack. Wangui Sherman, the owner of Bunivema Publishers—her mother's publisher—had invited him over to participate in the annual Bunivema Bookfest which had had to be put off. Ms. Sherman had however insisted that Dr. Agyeman would have loved for the launch to go on, as he believed so much in the continuity of life. The moment of silence was in honor of Kwasi Agyeman and the other sixty-four who had perished in the Eastend attack.

She looked around at the guests with their heads bowed in solemn silence. Even the governor of Nairobi was there! The press secretary from the Canadian embassy, who had come to present His Excellency the ambassador was also there. The Member of National Assembly for her rural home area was present too, as was the Cabinet Secretary for youth and sports. Someone had said that two other cabinet secretaries were expected. Bunivema Publishers had sent out most of the invites.

The minute of silence was over and the guests were formally invited by Wangui Sherman to the occasion and invited to help themselves to the available drinks and snacks as an accapella group entertained them. Carol drifted over to the corner where the drinks were and helped herself to a glass of white wine. She was eighteen now, legally an adult—with full privileges and liberties. She had joined the University of Nairobi just a couple of weeks earlier to study medical science, her long-time ambition.

"I will have a glass of that too," someone said towards her left. She swung around and faced Saidi.

"Whatever happened to 'the religion forbids it'?" she smiled teasingly.

"I won't get drunk and chase you into someone's house with a panga," he muttered from the corner of his mouth and they both sniggered quietly.

Now that the past was over, they could laugh about it. Saidi had grown sturdier and more muscular in the past couple of years. He now had a swarthy moustache and the dark outline of sideburns down each cheek. Carol thought he looked even more handsome than ever. He had won a scholarship to study computer science in Ontario, Canada and was due to join later that year. Just like Carol, he had scored an aggregate grade of A- in the final Kenya Certificate of Secondary Education examination the previous year with straight 'A's in Physics and Chemistry. Talking on the phone earlier in the day, Saidi had been so grateful to Carol for practically rescuing him from being recruited by the extremists. Perhaps he could easily have been one of those who carried out the attack on Eastend.

Carol's family had been able to move back to Nairobi soon after her mother's sudden recovery and Madam Juliet's discovery about her father's savings. With the savings, the money the government paid them for their share of land in the village and what they got from the out-of-court settlement over the demolition of their house, they had been able to purchase a spacious five-bedroomed house with a swimming pool and jacuzzi in Karen estate. Wangui Ndenga had put her creative instincts to action and transformed it into a beautiful residence. It was so masterfully decorated, furnished and painted that it resembled an enchanted palace straight off the pages of a children's storybook.

"Kaaro, please go and get some of the food for me," someone whispered into her ear.

It was Kadesa—a plumper, softer Kadesa. Her body had filled out and she was no longer so sharp-featured and painfully thin. She was wearing a beautiful *kitenge* dress with a matching headdress and smart, brown leather pumps. Carol and her mother had decided to take Kadesa and her children with them to the city and stay with them in their new home, where she now was their househelp. The woman was totally transformed, now that the tough, abusive life she had led was over.

"Tell Susy to give you some, I can see she is stuffing herself to the brim, she is not shy about food like you," Carol laughed, as she glanced to where Big Susy, dressed in a bright blue caftan that successfully hid her generous natural charms, was joyfully stuffing herself from an overflowing plate.

Carol's mother had helped Jemsi to get a driver's job with a company that ran factories in the Industrial Area and he now had a nice house out of the 'other Nairobi', which Big Susy had detested so much. She had now moved there with her children.

As Kadesa walked over to Big Susy, Carol excused herself to Saidi and went over to greet some of the other guest. In her flowing sea-green evening gown, and with her hair held up in an elegant coiffure, she looked grown-up and enchantingly beautiful, a younger replica of her mother. Soon it was time for Kui Ndenga to give her speech, and all attention turned to her. A large, plastic dummy of her book's cover graced the area near the podium.

"When my late husband Chris suddenly left us, I did not shed a single tear. I thought I had cried all the tears I could ever cry when my house was demolished. What I did not know was that I was holding stuff that I should have got out inside me. I did not know what to do. Chris had always taken such good care of us and I did not know where and how to start. Perhaps I was also too proud, or too angry or ashamed to ask for help. In the end, that was my undoing. My mind just imploded and shut down. But God had given me an angel to hold me up through those dark days–my daughter–Caroline, my firstborn."

Her voice broke a little with emotion before she valiantly went on.

"My daughter did everything I should have done, she made decisions and worked her fingers to the bone to take care of me and her siblings. God gave her the strength to carry all of us on her shoulders and be both mother and father to us all, although she was just a child. And in His good time, God engineered events in such a way that His will in our lives could come to pass.

I had never been very religious before, but now I am a firm believer in God's good time. If Carol's teacher had not asked her and her friend Saidi to do a chemistry project together at the school's science congress, perhaps they would never have paid Magwaro to help them, then he wouldn't have gotten drunk with the money and chased my good friend, Mabel—Kadesa, in the beautiful kitenge over there—into my hut in the village," she pointed and everyone turned to look at Kadesa, much to her consternation.

"The Bible says that God turns evil into good for His people and His glory and when His time comes, He will make things happen to fulfill His will. Now I believe that. My doctor says when I screamed my lungs out that evening, it acted as a catharsis that unblocked whatever had clogged up my mental functions and I was literally shocked back to my senses."

Many people in the audience laughed and some clapped before Kui went on.

"Many of you may not be aware that today is also Chris' fiftieth birthday—he was the same age as our nation. And so it is supposed to be his jubilee year too, during which as The Bible says, the captives are set free and what was lost restored. Chris may not be here to celebrate with us, but I'm sure he is happy as he watches over us from up there somewhere.

In my days of confusion, I was called 'song-of-birds' because I enjoyed the songs the birds sang and sang along with them. Even before that, I had been writing poems—most of them centred on birds and nature. Fortunately, I had saved them as drafts on my email account and I only had to work on them a bit more, with the help of the very, very talented Wangui Sherman and the wonderful people at Bunivema.

'A burst of Birdsong' is a celebration of nature and God's work, a kind of bird's eye-view of the simple things which we should be enjoying, yet we let them pass us by."

As she talked, Carol looked around and noticed more of the guests. Madam Juliet had not been able to make it. Her health was getting more delicate, but her daughter Lindsey, or Ondisa Chabuga-Walcott as she was officially known, had flown over.

She was standing to the left, in front of Carol. She looked stunning in her African print dress. She had indeed inherited the best of her dual heritage- creamy coffee-coloured skin , straight, brown hair and facial features that gave her a regal, queen-like commanding presence. She looked a little tense though. But there was no way Carol could know that it was because of what her mother had confided in her that morning over the phone. That the Ghanaian poet—Kwasi Agyeman— who had perished in the terrorist attack had been the son of Kwabena Agyeman, her mother's old flame.

Madam Juliet had been looking forward to meeting 'Benny's' son, and she was very much devastated by the turn of events, which was the main reason she hadn't come over as she had wanted to. Ondisa was in the process of changing the name of Hillside Academy into 'The Hezbon Chabuga Educational Centre' at her mother's request. Madam Juliet wanted the school to be her late husband's memorial, and she had willed her entire possessions to it. It was to be relocated to more spacious grounds in the course of the next year.

Carol's attention turned back to her mother and her speech.

"I'm honored to also have here a friend of Carol's, Saidi Salim, who may someday be my son in-law."

At this, Carol blushed.

"I am very proud of Salim for choosing right over wrong, love over hate. We are all children of the universe. Every one of us has every right to be here and none of us has the right to take away another's life for whatever reason. Saidi could have been one of those who carried out that horrible, ungodly act at Eastend, but he refused to be forced into doing what he knew was wrong. He ran away, with the help of friends, from the home he had always known rather than be taught to hate and kill, to join a murderous organization."

Carol found herself searching with her eyes for Saidi among the guests. She spotted him grinning to himself near where the buffet had been laid. "The rascal... so proud of himself—thinks he is so important..." she thought as she looked at him fondly. The fact was that she was also very proud of him. He had made a report to the anti-terror unit of the police and Mustafa and his henchmen had eventually been arrested. They were still in police custody helping with investigations into terrorism activities in the country. Carol secretly thought Saidi was a hero. HER hero.

Glossary

Akala	-	sandals made from old car tires
Alhamdulillah	-	may God be praised
Amaga	-	cracks that form on calloused heels
Assalam aleikum	-	An Arabic greeting meaning 'peace be with you'
Baya!	-	a word used as an admonition or to express surprise
Buibuis	-	long black dresses usually worn by Muslim women
Chang'aa	-	a traditional gin
Chapatti	-	unleavened wheat bread
Fundi	-	any craftsman, in this case the mason
Githeri	-	a boiled mixture of maize and beans
Haki	-	really
Haya	-	okay
Hijab	-	a scarf usually worn around the head by Muslim girls and women
Inshallah	-	God willing.
Kafir	-	an Arabic term meaning 'unbeliever'. Here, it is used in an insulting way.
Kanzu	-	a long garment worn by men
Karai	-	a metal basin
Kifwaavi	-	mess or abomination
Kitenge	-	a colourful, patterned fabric common in East, West and Central Africa
Kufumbika	-	preserving a burning ember of fire by

	heaping ashes around it to stop it from going out
Leso/khanga	- cotton wrappers that are usually colourfully dyed
Lwa-Manyonyi	- song of birds...the full phrase should be 'lwimbu lwa manyonyi'
Mabati	- iron sheets
Magu	- Man! Exclamation of surprise or wonderment
Mandazi	- a type of bun
Matatu	- public transport vehicles
Mjengo	- building/ construction site
Murenda	- jute greens
Mzungu	- white person
Ngai	- an exclamation of surprise (God!)
Panga	- matchet or cutlass
Piizuri	- a mispronunciation of 'P3'
Serikali	- the government
Sisemi kitu	- I have no comment.
Sukuma-wiki	- a type of kale
Ugali	- maize flour cooked into a form of stiff porridge
Uluhya/oluhya/oluyia	- a sitting of elders.
Vibarua	- casual jobs
Vusaasu	- wood splinters
Woiyee	- a slang term used to express pity or sympathy

NOTE: Most of the words depicted as the songs of birds are mostly onomatopoeic and do not have any real sensible meaning.

www.ingramcontent.com/pod-product-compliance
Lightning Source LLC
LaVergne TN
LVHW041948070526
838199LV00051BA/2945